SPECIAL MESSAGE TO READERS

THE ULVERSCROFT FOUNDATION
(registered UK charity number 264873)

was established in 1972 to provide funds for research, diagnosis and treatment of eye diseases. Examples of major projects funded by the Ulverscroft Foundation are:-

- The Children's Eye Unit at Moorfields Eye Hospital, London
- The Ulverscroft Children's Eye Unit at Great Ormond Street Hospital for Sick Children
- Funding research into eye diseases and treatment at the Department of Ophthalmology, University of Leicester
- The Ulverscroft Vision Research Group, Institute of Child Health
- Twin operating theatres at the Western Ophthalmic Hospital, London
- The Chair of Ophthalmology at the Royal Australian College of Ophthalmologists

You can help further the work of the Foundation by making a donation or leaving a legacy. Every contribution is gratefully received. If you would like to help support the Foundation or require further information, please contact:

THE ULVERSCROFT FOUNDATION
The Green, Bradgate Road, Anstey
Leicester LE7 7FU, England
Tel: (0116) 236 4325

website: www.foundation.ulverscroft.com

RETURN TO RIVER SPRINGS

Nine years ago Georgia left River Springs, vowing never to return. But now she's back to start a new job — only to discover that the secrets of her past will not stay buried. Before she has a chance to reconcile with her old flame, Detective Justin Rose, an accident lands her daughter in hospital; and when morning comes, the little girl is nowhere to be found. With her life falling apart around her, and Justin demanding answers she doesn't want to give, Georgia begins the desperate search for her daughter . . .

Books by Charlotte McFall
in the Linford Romance Library:

HEALING THE HURT
DIFFICULT DECISIONS

CHARLOTTE McFALL

RETURN TO RIVER SPRINGS

Complete and Unabridged

LINFORD
Leicester

First published in Great Britain in 2016

First Linford Edition
published 2016

A catalogue record for this book is available
from the British Library.

ISBN 978–1–4448–2984–6

Published by
F. A. Thorpe (Publishing)
Anstey, Leicestershire

Set by Words & Graphics Ltd.
Anstey, Leicestershire
Printed and bound in Great Britain by
T. J. International Ltd., Padstow, Cornwall

This book is printed on acid-free paper

1

'You okay, little one?' Georgia pulled her daughter to her for a hug before they climbed the steps to the school.

'Sure, Mom.' Misty smiled up at her. 'Don't worry. I can do this.'

Georgia smiled. 'I know you can, hun. But it's my job to worry about you.'

'There's no need, Mom. I'll be just fine.' Misty's upturned face was endearingly earnest. 'This looks like a nice school.'

'It does. Let's go get you registered.'

Misty took her hand and gave it a squeeze. 'This one might be a keeper.'

The innocent comment pulled at Georgia's heart. This was the fourth grade-school Misty had attended, and she knew that Misty craved nothing more than to stay put for more than just a few months. Georgia wanted that too, so much, but she wasn't as optimistic as her daughter that River Springs was the place they would settle. She had history in this town. Secrets, too.

'Let's hope so, Misty.'

★ ★ ★

Georgia pulled into the parking lot of the police station. It was 8:05 a.m. and she was early for her first day at work. Misty was happily ensconced in the breakfast club at her new school, and Georgia was two for two on her to-do list.

She understood the building was new, but the building supplies taking up four parking spaces were testament to just how new. When she'd last been in town, Maxine's Department Store was the only building above three stories. The station looked to have at least four.

There was no other car in the parking lot, and when Georgia approached the entrance, the area was unlit. If she hadn't just taken Misty to school, she would have sworn she'd gotten the wrong day to start her current assignment. She pushed the 'open' button for the automatic door, but it didn't work. The door wasn't locked; it rattled in its frame as she tested it. She pushed her way in and paused, waiting for an alarm to sound. Nothing.

The reception floor was highly polished, and protective plastic matting indicated a preferred walkway to the meet-and-greet desk, again unmanned. Georgia began to have doubts this was where she was supposed to be. She was to meet the boss in the boardroom at nine o'clock, according to the emailed schedule from Neason's Head Office, and this was the address she'd been given.

With a shrug, Georgia leaned across the waist-high desk and found a sign-in book. The most recent visitors were apparently tradesmen, given the business names. Scrawling her own name, she carefully put the book back, shouldered her briefcase, and looked for directions to the conference room. Third floor, according to the sign on the wall, which was still covered with sticky plastic protection. The elevator should be right around the corner; the sign was propped on a pile of tiles against the wall. Georgia summoned it and felt naughty leaving a fingerprint on the brushed aluminum.

She stepped into what felt like the smallest elevator she had seen and pressed the button for the third floor. She checked her reflection in the mirrored interior, catching the same wide-eyed expression she'd seen on her daughter's face earlier. Misty had been a bit nervous starting a new school, but then she was used to it, they moved so often.

The light flickered, momentary darkness hiding Georgia's twin image, and she held on to the handrail as a whining noise began. The elevator stopped moving, an alarm sounded, and dull red emergency lighting blinked into life.

4

Oh, come on! Georgia waited to see if the machinery would kick back in automatically, but nothing happened. No one noticed — but then, they wouldn't; there was no one here. Her phone buzzed with the next scheduled item on her list, but she dismissed it with a swipe of her finger. Getting stuck wasn't on her agenda. She dialed the number she had programmed into her phone over the weekend, listening to a ringing signal and then a recorded message.

'Thank you for calling River Springs Police and Justice Department. The department is currently closed. If you have an emergency, please dial 911. Our opening hours are Monday to Friday, nine a.m. to five p.m. If you know the extension of the person you wish to speak to, press one. If you'd like to leave a message, press two.'

Great! She wasn't sure getting stuck in an elevator on the first day in her new job constituted an emergency. She'd just have to sit it out. Someone would want the elevator sooner or later. She kicked off her shoes and sat down. It would give her a bit more time to go over her presentation and proposal for the River Springs Police and Justice Department's move to Sentinel's software.

Georgia was engrossed in her projected savings spreadsheet and didn't notice the grinding sound at first, not until it became louder. The noise, and the vibrations shaking the elevator, set her teeth on edge. Scrambling to her knees, she pressed the emergency call button, waiting while it buzzed. It was past nine o'clock; someone had to be in the building by now.

'What's your emergency?' the operator answered.

Georgia frowned. What was up with this building? 'I'm trapped in an elevator at the police station.'

'Which police station, ma'am? You're speaking to River Springs Police — '

'The very same. Can someone come get me out?'

'I'm sorry, ma'am, but the River Springs Police Station doesn't have an elevator.'

'I'm in the new building, the Police and Justice — '

'One moment, ma'am. Patching you through to the new dispatch office. It's not open yet, but they're in the same building as you.'

Georgia heard a muffled exchange of words through the console, followed by: 'Ms. Baxter? This is Detective Rose. Are you okay in there?' The tone of his voice was curt. Georgia's breath caught in her throat.

'Yes.' She swallowed nervously, her mouth dry.

'Sit tight; we'll get you out as soon as we can.' There was silence, apart from the thud of Georgia's heart in her ears. Justin? She hadn't been expecting that. Her boss had told her that she would be meeting with a Detective King.

She sat back against the wall and picked up her laptop, but she couldn't get her eyes to focus on the screen;

unexpected tears blurred her vision. The red light was not conducive to working on a computer, she told herself, and it was getting extremely hot in here. She checked her phone again. Nine-thirty a.m. There had been no fresh air circulating for over an hour; that was why her head was now aching. 'Breathe,' she whispered.

It wasn't a panic attack, at least not one caused by being stuck in the smallest elevator ever. It was more to do with the man she'd just spoken to. The man she'd left in the middle of the night, nine years ago.

Georgia heard a further scrape of metal on metal and a muttered curse, and the elevator doors parted. The man who she had kidded herself must have moved on from River Springs was now on his hands and knees, looking through a twelve-inch gap at her.

'You okay?' The sound of his deep voice echoed around the small space.

Georgia nodded, her teeth firmly biting the inside of her lower lip. She didn't trust herself to speak.

'You're gonna have to crawl out. The elevator's between floors. The gears are stuck and they can't get it moving.' Justin Rose put his arm through the gap, his palm open. 'Take my hand.'

Georgia looked at his arm. His shirt sleeve was rolled up, and she saw a silver metal watch on his wrist. He reached in further, his fingertips grazing her arm.

'I can't fit through there!'

'Are you packing some extra pounds these days?'

He'd been teasing the last time he'd asked her that, the same evening she'd left him. She'd just gotten out of the shower, wrapped in one of the new fluffy towels they'd bought that afternoon. She'd been standing at the vanity unit looking in the mirror as Justin squeezed behind her, pausing to drop a kiss on her exposed shoulder. He'd pressed himself against her and wrapped his arms around her waist for a hug. Georgia had been so pleased that she'd found such thick towels in the department store, and he'd teased her, asking the same question, knowing full well his fingers felt her curves through the plush material.

His face appeared in the gap now and his gaze swept over her. 'Nope, didn't think so. Come on!'

'My things — '

'Can stay there until they sort the problem out.'

'My presentation — '

'You can't do your job without a computer?' Georgia heard him mutter something as he thrust his head and shoulders fully into the gap. 'Now, give me your hand. I can't wait all day for you. I have a job to do, and so do you.'

★ ★ ★

Georgia was pulled unceremoniously through a tiny gap, and scrambled to a sitting position against the wall. She looked around, unable to concentrate on any one thing. There were clearly more people here than there had been earlier; quite a crowd had gathered. What must she look like? Georgia glanced down to see two buttons missing from her blouse, and her shoes were also gone. It looked like she'd walked barefoot to work.

A paramedic knelt on one side of her, fingers on her wrist checking her pulse. 'Do you suffer from asthma or any other conditions, ma'am?' Georgia shook her head at the same time as another paramedic attached an oxygen mask to her face. 'Do you remember what happened? Have you suffered any blows to the head?' She shook her head again, her eyes wide, looking around the group of bystanders for Detective Rose.

He was deep in conversation with a woman who was highly animated, pointing alternately between Georgia and a clipboard. Her blonde curls bobbed as she did all of the talking. Justin glanced Georgia's way, rubbing his hand along his jaw. Some things didn't change; he always did that when he was thinking, weighing up a situation. Georgia wondered what the woman was saying. She was kind of familiar, but Georgia couldn't remember anyone she knew from all those years ago who fit her appearance.

'Your vitals seem fine. If you're feeling okay, we'll let you get on with your day.'

Georgia returned her attention to the paramedics, who removed the mask and stood smiling over her. She'd forgotten how easily good manners came to the people here. 'Thank you.'

'It's no problem, ma'am. Have a good day.'

As they left, Justin headed toward Georgia, closely followed by the blonde, who stopped in her tracks as he put a hand out and shook his head.

'Ms. Baxter.' Justin stood over her, holding out his hand as if he was greeting her formally for the first time, rather than having all but manhandled her out of the elevator. Georgia blushed as he helped her to her feet. 'I hope this hasn't put you off working with us at River Springs station.'

'You can't help the fact your elevator isn't functioning correctly, Detective Rose,' came her pleasant reply.

He gave her a friendly smile. 'Actually, the elevator's not supposed to be functioning, period. The building's not due to open until next Monday. I'm surprised you managed to get in here at all.'

'But we were due to meet here at nine a.m.,' Georgia floundered, her fingers curling around the phone in her trouser pocket. She pulled it out and saw the screen was cracked, probably from when Justin had pulled her out of the elevator. 'The email said nine a.m., in the board room at the Police and Justice Department, Sea Island Drive, River Springs.' She scrolled down the email and thrust it at Justin's face.

'If you'd read it properly, you would have noted my instructions to meet *outside*, so we could sign in, put the appropriate personal protective equipment on and tour the new building, before convening in the conference room for your presentation.' He pushed the phone aside with one finger.

Georgia swallowed and could see the blonde hovering a few feet away, almost hopping from foot to foot, dying to get in on the conversation. She tried to concentrate on Justin, whose passive face gave nothing away, but the woman kept drawing her attention. Justin followed Georgia's gaze and the blonde took the opportunity to join them. 'Our legal team will want us to initiate an internal investigation into how Ms. Baxter was able to gain access to the building today,' she said. The woman's tone was officious and she didn't acknowledge Georgia's presence.

'I simply came to work early,' Georgia told her.

'Sneaking around seems to be your forte,' the blonde muttered.

'I wanted to be prepared. Is that a crime?'

The blonde's lips curled in disdain. 'Unlawful entry is a crime. We'd be well within our rights to prosecute; and then there's the wanton disregard for the department's health and safety procedures.' Her voice became louder. 'As an employee of River Springs Police and — '

'I'm not employed by River Springs.' Georgia squared her shoulders and turned to face the shorter woman.

'Ladies, please.' Justin's voice was loud enough to stop them both in their tracks. 'Karen, we'll talk about what needs to be done later, thank you. Ms. Baxter's had quite an ordeal this morning and I'm sure she'd like a moment to collect herself.' He looked pointedly at Karen.

'Yes, boss.' Karen's response was as professional as Justin's, and she left them, but not before she narrowed her eyes at Georgia. 'Ms. Baxter.'

A thoughtful frown creased Georgia's forehead. 'Karen?' she said, turning to Justin.

'Yes.'

'Karen, as in Karen and Paul?'

'The same. Why?'

'They both work in the same department now?'

'No, Paul doesn't work here any-more.'

Georgia wanted to ask more, but Justin's frown didn't encourage it. Instead, Georgia smiled. 'She looks so different. I didn't know her that well anyway, but she looks great.'

'You should tell her; she'd appreciate it. She worked hard to lose weight.'

'Things sure have changed in River Springs. New police station, new Karen.' Georgia shook her head in disbelief.

'Did you think time stood still after you'd gone?' Justin's voice was low enough that only she could hear it. She looked up at him to see if his expression had changed. It was the first time he'd said anything about her leaving. But if the frown had deepened with his words, it was gone in an instant, and the friendly smile was back in place.

'Justin, I'm — '

'Let me show you where the restroom is. I'm sure you'd like a few minutes.' He moved away. She closed her eyes for a split second before following him. He clearly didn't want to talk about anything related to their past, and Georgia mentally ticked off the imaginary item from her to-do list — 'Tell Justin you're sorry for running out on him. He might forgive you. He might want you back. He might still love you.'

That clearly wasn't going to happen.

★ ★ ★

Georgia cleaned herself up and was reunited with her shoes, but the buttons were still missing. She meant to go home at some point and change, but hadn't had chance yet; Justin had given her a tour of the new building, including the new control room, where Karen watched her like a hawk.

Justin explained that Karen was the facilities manager and oversaw not only the building but also the resourcing of the dispatch room. He wanted Georgia to work with Karen during her assessment to see how the Sentinel software could best be configured to work with existing systems. That was going to be fun. She felt she was already on strike two with Karen, for alleged unlawful entry. What she couldn't figure out was what the first strike was for — it was clear Karen had had an agenda before they'd even spoken. Georgia had an uncomfortable feeling it was something to do with leaving Justin. What that had to do directly with the woman, Georgia wasn't sure, but she wasn't looking forward to finding out.

They finally broke for coffee in the conference room, and Georgia felt she was back on familiar ground, her equilibrium regained following her adventures of the morning. She gave her presentation on how Sentinel worked for other law enforcement agencies across the country, and said how she looked forward to working closely with the River Springs team. She wrapped up the demonstration of the software and opened the floor for questions. Karen jumped straight in without putting her hand up.

'I've been looking at Neason's website to see what other police forces across the country have been forced to make changes to their already effective working practices.' Georgia waited for the rest with a polite smile. 'I spoke to a counterpart over in Jefferson County, who gave me the impression that they were forced into using Neason's without a proper analysis of their existing systems. Is that how you work?'

Talk about rude! Georgia was just about to answer when Justin's cell phone rang, along with the phones of a few other people in the room. 'Big road traffic accident between two vehicles on the highway,' he said. 'Let's get the appropriate teams on site. Karen, please set up a control room at the site with the mobile units and assign a liaison officer to work with the other services.'

Georgia noted the authority in his voice and the immediate effect it had on his team. They knew what they were expected to do and had no need to question his directions. As people stood and left the room, Georgia wondered what she should do while they were all gone. Justin stood at the head of the table, both hands resting on the wooden surface.

'I want you to come along with me, to observe,' Justin told her. 'This is a serious incident, and you'll get a good understanding of the type of information we're using to coordinate a rapid response. Are you up for it?'

Georgia swallowed hard, her throat tight, but she spoke calmly. The seriousness of the call was not lost on her. 'Of course. What should I bring?'

'Nothing. It's purely for observation. Leave everything here; you can collect it later. Let's get you a high-visibility jacket. It'll say 'observer' on it, so no one will expect you to be doing anything.'

As he spoke, Justin rounded the table and ushered her out of the conference room, his hand on the small of her back. Georgia tried not to be aware of the firm pressure guiding her down the stairs and out of the building. She tried not to think about the warmth of his hand through the thin material of her business suit. But it was there, and in the closed environs of his police car she was hyper-aware of his presence.

The frequency used by the emergency services was full of chatter. Georgia knew that Justin was listening but also concentrating on driving the car, weaving his way through the downtown River Springs lunchtime traffic, lights flashing and sirens blaring. She wanted to talk to him, to break the silence between them, but didn't want to interrupt his concentration.

While he was an expert driver, Georgia couldn't help but feel a little nauseous due to the way the car was nipping from side to side as Justin negoted a safe path. Her parents had died in a car crash when she was sixteen, and she'd been wary of getting in cars where she wasn't in control ever since. She hadn't had a feeling like this in years. Perhaps attending the scene of an accident wasn't such a good plan. She felt like someone had pulled the plug on her stomach; it was sinking fast.

Justin finished calling in his ETA to the dispatch office. Georgia looked pale, her knuckles white where she was gripping the seatbelt.

'Am I driving too fast?'

She turned to look at him, her eyes wide, and shook her head.

Her parents! How had he forgotten that one? 'Are you okay, Georgia?'

She never talked about her parents. She answered with a nod this time, and Justin returned his attention to the road. She'd been back in his life for just a few hours and had already made her mark — and that was only from getting stuck in the elevator. He certainly didn't want to get involved with her in any way other than professionally. But when she looked at him with those green eyes . . .

'We're here.' He parked the car and reached into the back seat, pulling out safety vests for both of them. 'Put this on, and you'll need a hard hat too.' He didn't suppose there was much danger of her getting crowned by a falling object, but protocol was there for a reason. It didn't seem that she had much respect for rules and regulations if this morning was anything to go by.

He saw her check the wording on the back of the jacket and then shrug it on. She kept up with him as he wound his way around the safety cordon to where a group of emergency professionals were gathered.

'Rose.' The fire boss nodded to him, clapping his shoulder.

'Boss.' Justin nodded. 'What have we got?'

'The school bus skidded and flipped.

It's on its roof in a pool of fuel. We need to get the kids out as soon as the crews have made the spillage safe.'

'Any idea how it happened?' Justin asked him.

'Witness says the tanker failed to stop at the red light, skidded and rolled over. The bus driver was thrown clear through the windscreen on impact, and the tanker driver is trapped. The fire crew is working on cutting him out; he's in a bad way.'

'Any fatalities?'

'Only one that we know of so far.' The paramedic in charge consulted his notebook. 'Pedestrian, an old man who was crossing the road. He was caught by the front of the tanker. Would have been instant.'

'Thanks. Just to let you know, we're being observed today by Ms. Baxter. Georgia, it's probably best if you stay behind the cordon.'

Georgia nodded, trying to take everything in. The wreckage of the two vehicles was awful and she could hear the children crying. The smell of the spilled fuel was almost overwhelming. Her eyes stung. The fire crews suiting up to deal with the incident were also putting on breathing apparatus. In the haze of the early afternoon, the vapor was clear to see.

Justin motioned for her to follow him. 'In the tent over there, Karen will be coordinating contact between the services and liaising with the hospital, advising them on the number of casualties that'll be arriving. Record-keeping is essential.'

'How long has Karen been in the post?' Georgia walked faster to match Justin's long strides.

'Five years or so.'

'She seemed resentful, this morning and in the briefing.' It was out of her mouth before she knew it and Justin stopped.

'You want to do this now?' he said, incredulous.

'If we're going to work together, I need to know what her problem is,

Justin. I need to know what I can expect.'

'Karen is scared that this new system will put her and her team out of a job. Is that problem enough?'

A fleeting sensation of relief shot through Georgia. Thankfully it was professional rather than personal. She'd dealt with concerns like this before on other projects. Karen was just worried for herself and her team, for obvious reasons. Not everyone coped well with change, and for some people it was a really frightening thing. For others it felt like a personal slight, as if their work wasn't good enough.

'It'll help the department to work in a more cohesive way,' Georgia said. 'It isn't really a problem.' She gave her best reassuring smile, but Justin remained po-faced. 'I'm sure we'll get along fine when she understands.'

'Oh, and she thinks you were way out of line for walking out on me,' he added, before turning away from her.

Georgia's whole body flushed with

mortification. She stood and stared, open-mouthed, at his retreating back. He wasn't even talking about his own feelings; surely that was yet to come. Would she be ready for the accusations and finger-pointing?

Justin had reached the temporary command center and was talking to Karen at the entrance. They both glanced over to Georgia and he waved her over.

How was she supposed to face Karen now? *Be professional, that's how.* Georgia moved slowly; the spread of the fuel had nearly reached the cordon now and she didn't want to slip on it. She'd caused more than enough trouble already.

She was just about level with the upended school bus some sixty feet away. Some of the children were screaming for their parents; she could see their little faces pressed against the windows. There were already some parents at the scene, straining at the cordon to get a glance of their precious babies. Bad news certainly did travel fast in this small community. She felt for them. What would she do if it had been Misty?

Georgia was nearing the command center when her phone buzzed with a text. Her hand was in her pocket before she saw Justin's frown.

'Turn your phone off, Georgia. The fuel is highly flammable. It'd only take one spark!' His voice was urgent and firm, but her fingers were automatically pressing 'open message' on the screen.

Her eyes scanned the text; it was from Misty's school. Her class had been on an outing — Georgia remembered being told that at the school earlier that morning; she'd had to sign a permission form. Misty had thought it was so cool that they were going to the River Springs nature reserve on her first day. The morning already seemed like days ago. There'd been an accident, the message said. The school bus had been in a collision. The emergency services were already on scene. Parents were advised to meet at the school, where they would be kept informed.

Georgia started to shake as she looked from the message to the school bus. Misty. Misty was on the bus. 'Misty!' she whispered, stepping closer to the cordon. She didn't need to be at the school. She was here, where her baby was one of the children trapped in the bus.

'Georgia, what are you doing? Turn the phone off and move back. You're compromising everyone's safety.' Justin was at her side, his hand on her wrist.

'Misty. She's on the bus.'

'Georgia, who's Misty?' He tried to pull her back.

'My daughter.' Her voice rose, a sob trapped in her throat. 'Misty's on the bus!'

Justin had his arms around her waist, restraining her as she tried to move forward to get to the bus. 'Georgia, if she's in there, let the firefighters do their job. It'll be okay. You can't go in there.'

Georgia was determined to get to her daughter, calling her name over and over.

'Georgia! Stop!' Justin picked her up and bodily moved her to the command center.

'Justin, let me go. Justin, please?' Georgia was crying now, begging as he set her on the ground, but he didn't release his hold on her. As her feet touched the ground she braced herself against Justin's grip, her hands pushing at his as she tried to break free.

'Georgia — '

'Let me go. Let go!' she yelled. He didn't understand. Why was he trying to stop her getting to her baby? Fear made her stronger, and she tore at his hands. She drove her elbows into his ribs. She kicked at his legs. She twisted and wriggled.

'For Pete's sake, will you stop?' He held her tighter. Georgia felt her ribcage against her arms.

A loud whoosh and intense heat grabbed their attention. The fuel had ignited and the fire was headed for the bus.

'Misty!' Georgia screamed as the tanker exploded into flames.

2

Georgia rocked on her feet from the force of the explosion, upright only because Justin held her so close. Her scream died in her throat and her tears dried on her face from the heat of the blast.

It happened so quickly. The tanker caught fire just as the fire crew finished dousing the bus in foam, protecting it from the worst of the heat. A wall of energy pushed the bus further away, almost righting it as it came to rest against a street sign, which buckled under the weight.

Georgia's knees buckled under the weight of her fear. Without a word, Justin picked her up and walked to the tent, putting her down in a chair. Her body was numb, shock cutting the signals from her brain to her legs. She heard Justin talking to Karen, but her eyes were focused on the scene outside.

'Georgia's daughter is on the bus,' he said.

'Daughter?' Karen mouthed.

He shrugged, giving Georgia's hand a squeeze. 'I won't be long.' Then he left, his radio to his ear as he listened to updates, and Karen sat beside her.

'What's your daughter's name?' Karen asked, trying to engage her, but Georgia couldn't refocus her eyes.

'Misty.'

'How old is she?'

'Eight.' Georgia remembered Misty saying she couldn't wait until her next birthday in a couple of months' time, because nine was so much older than eight.

Karen's hand covered Georgia's. 'The crews are just getting the kids out now. According to the teachers on board, everyone is alive.'

A sob caught in Georgia's throat. 'Oh, thank God.'

'Can I get you something to drink?' Karen stood.

'No, I'm fine. I just want to know that Misty's okay.'

'Sure.' Karen took an incoming call on her radio.

'Karen.'

'Yes, boss?'

'Get a list of everyone on that bus.'

'I have it already, boss. The school emailed it a few minutes ago. You want a copy?'

'Sure. I'll be back in a few minutes. Out.'

Georgia was still but for her fingers working against each other, unsure of what she should be doing. Justin told her to wait. Karen told her to wait. But didn't her daughter need her? Shouldn't she be out there, helping, doing something?

Karen pressed a cup of coffee into her shaking hands. 'I don't know how you take it, but it's all we've got at the moment. Catering's not the most important thing at a crime scene.'

Karen's joke fell short of the mark. 'Is it a crime scene?' Georgia frowned.

'I thought it was an accident.'

'The wrong phrase.' Karen smiled apologetically. 'An investigation will take place to determine the cause of the accident and then, depending on the findings, there may be a prosecution. But that's a while down the road yet.'

Georgia took a sip of the hot, bitter liquid. 'Thanks for the coffee.'

Justin returned and took a pile of papers from Karen. He glanced at Georgia before focusing on the list. Sure enough, highlighted in green were the words 'Misty Baxter, Third Grade.'

'She said the girl is eight,' Karen whispered.

'Yeah, thanks, Karen, I figured that out for myself.' Justin's tone was sharper than he'd intended, if the look on her face was anything to go by. 'Third grade.' He pointed to the page.

Karen's face relaxed. 'How are you feeling, boss? Can I get you a coffee?'

'A coffee would be great, but it'll have to wait. I'm going to see if I can be of any use with the rescue. Look after her for me?' He nodded his head in Georgia's direction. Karen raised her eyebrows and Justin shook his head. 'Don't make anything of it,' he warned in a low voice.

He walked toward the fire boss, considering Karen's question. How was he feeling? It certainly hadn't been the day he'd planned. When he'd heard that Sentinel was sending Georgia Baxter to work with him, his gut reaction had been to call the whole thing off. He didn't need that particular complication back in his life, not after nine years without her. But the professional in him knew the software could rationalize the way his department worked.

He knew he was bound to have some sort of reaction to Georgia's return, but he had tried not to think about it too much. He had all but sealed off that part of his life; those six months she'd been in his world were now a blur. Georgia had had an effect on him instantly, the first time they met and she crashed her trolley into him in the produce aisle at the supermarket. If today was anything to go by, she hadn't changed one bit.

It had been an eventful start to the week. Still, he was just doing his job — even if that job was rescuing Georgia from an elevator or her daughter from a wreck. The fact remained that he and Georgia had a thing many years ago, but then she'd left. He'd gotten over it. Life carried on, regardless of any pain, and other people came and went. There were still unanswered questions, but the world hadn't ended. The look on Georgia's face, however, showed that her world *had* almost ended today.

Justin switched his mind to the job at hand. 'Boss, can I work alongside the crew? Thought you could use another pair of hands.'

The fire boss nodded and pointed to a team getting suited up in additional PPE, getting ready to get into the bus. 'Suit up, Rose. The boys have contained the tanker fire, but there's a lot of gasoline on the ground and we're not sure what the state of the bus engine is. Where the bus landed on its roof there's structural damage to the supporting pillars, and the windshield has folded but not cracked.'

'Any priority patients to get off first?' A name in green highlighter pen flashed in his mind's eye. He shook his head quickly to clear the image.

'No new casualties since the explosion flipped the bus right side up, but a couple of the kids got thrown around, so not sure until we get in there.'

Justin joined the crew, who were figuring out the best way to get into the vehicle, wiping the thick foam away with their gloved hands. As the foam slid down the windows, the viscous mixture thinned and left streaks. Justin could see a child looking out, tears on her face, her fear clear as day. He could hear the teachers on the bus trying to keep the kids calm by singing songs, but the girl at the window wasn't joining in. Could she be Georgia's daughter?

Keep your mind on the job, Rose! Justin gritted his teeth as he shucked on the breathing apparatus that his colleagues were wearing — a precaution, but essential for their own safety. The little girl had gone and he pushed the image of her scared face from his mind.

Two firefighters were ready with the Jaws of Life, cutting the pillars at the rear of the vehicle. The vibrating shears ground against the twisted metal as shining splinters flew through the air. Justin shielded his face against the shards and suddenly noticed the friction of the shears against the bus sending tiny sparks into the air. They'd no doubt fizzle out before they got anywhere near the foam-drenched gasoline on the tarmac, but there was no telling whether the fumes had yet dissipated.

Justin touched one of the shear operators firmly on the shoulder and waited until he had the man's attention. He then extended a finger on one hand and pinched his index finger and thumb together and opened them to indicate the spark. The operator watched his signal carefully, nodded and then repeated the same to his colleague, waving his palm horizontally in front of his throat, indicating for him to stop.

The firefighter cut the power to the machinery, applied the safety guard and stepped back out of the circle of men.

'What's up?' the fire boss called to Justin.

'Sparks. Don't want to risk another blast, boss.'

'Try the hydraulic spreaders; you've cut far enough through the column.' The fire crew followed their boss's instructions without hesitation.

As the powerful spreaders opened the back of the bus bit by bit, Justin grasped an edge of the jagged metal, grateful for the supreme grip his heavy leather gloves gave him. It didn't matter how many times he saw these firefighters in action at the scene of an accident; their strength and determination made him proud to call these men colleagues.

Together they peeled back the pliable metal an inch at a time, the spreaders doing what they were designed to do. They used manual shears to cut along the base of the rear panel of the bus, separating it from the floor. The rescuers pushed the two halves of the panel wide open, and Justin could see the teachers had moved the kids further toward the front of the bus.

The noise of the machinery had scared the kids even more, and some of them were whimpering, while others sobbed. Justin looked around for the little girl who'd been at the window but couldn't find her.

Satisfied the bus was safe for the paramedics to come aboard, the fire-fighters carefully lifted out the frightened children and put them on the gurneys that had been wheeled within ten feet of the bus. Justin threaded his way up the aisle, checking that those who could move independently did so, and stepped aside for a colleague to pass. His leg brushed something sticking out from one of the seats and he looked down with a frown.

'My leg!' The girl from the window winced in pain, her teeth biting hard on her lower lip. 'My leg hurts.'

'Let's get you out of here, hun. We'll get a doctor to check out your leg. Are you hurt anywhere else?' He stooped down next to the seat, careful not to knock her foot again.

She turned her head to show a nasty gash on her forehead and blood smeared into her hair. Her teeth sank into her lip again as Justin lifted the hair from her face.

'Okay, darlin', I'm going to lift you out of the seat. I'll try not to hurt you too much, but we need to get you out of here.' He kept his voice calm and quiet and she responded, a small hand gripping his jacket as he leaned in, carefully sliding one arm under her legs and one around her waist. He lifted her with ease, sensing her pain, her upper body tense as she tried to hold herself still. He held her as tightly as he could without hurting her.

As he stepped gently down from the back of the bus, the descent jarred the girl's leg. He saw swelling on her shin as a broken bone pressed hard against the pale skin. She flinched and cried out as the ragged end of the fibula pierced her flesh. She passed out from the pain and shock, tears running through the soot on her cheeks.

Justin rushed to the gurney as blood poured from the open wound. At least the little girl wouldn't feel anything for a while. A paramedic pushed the wheeled bed flat as Justin laid her down carefully. 'What have we got?'

'I suspect a broken fibula, just pierced the skin now. Poor kid passed out. She's got a head wound, but she was conscious and talking up until thirty seconds ago. I couldn't see any other injuries. I got her out of there as fast as I could.'

One paramedic made an initial assessment of the girl's vitals; another approached Justin with a clipboard. 'Do you know her name?'

'No.'

A woman sitting on a gurney nearby removed her oxygen mask to speak. 'That's the new girl. She just started today.'

'At the school?' the paramedic asked.

'I can't remember her name.' The woman coughed and returned the mask to her face.

'Misty,' Justin whispered at the same time the medic found the girls' name on the list.

'Could it be Misty Baxter?' the medic asked the woman, who nodded, and he ticked Misty off the list. 'We'll take her to the emergency room and we'll liaise with the school from there. They sent a text to tell parents to gather there, but a lot of them are already at the hospital.'

Justin glanced at the girl, her face pale beneath the soot, eyelashes dark against her skin. 'Her mother's here. Can you wait while I go get her?'

'Be quick. We need to get the bone

realigned, but not here. She's losing blood.'

'Sure.' Justin headed straight for the command center, his fire helmet in his hands. Georgia looked up as he entered. He couldn't remember ever seeing her so scared.

'Misty?' Her voice cracked as she spoke.

'She's getting ready to go to the hospital. I asked the paramedics to wait.'

'Is she okay?' She stood up, Justin's nod not settling her thoughts. 'I need to see her.'

He nodded again and she followed him under the cordon. He walked fast, but adrenaline kept her apace of him. As they headed to where her daughter was being attended, he said, 'Broken leg, not sure how severe it is, and a cut to her head. She lost consciousness when she got off the bus.' He halted and put his hand out to stop Georgia from walking ahead. 'Georgia, just to warn you, the bone has penetrated the skin. You were always squeamish, and — '

Georgia flashed him a look, her tone sharp as she snapped, 'She's my daughter. Squeamish doesn't cut it anymore. I got over that a long time ago.'

'She's just through here.'

Georgia tried to see through the small crowd gathered around and then spotted Misty, supine on the trolley, oxygen mask on her face, saline IV in her arm, a splint on her left leg from thigh to ankle, and her eyes closed. The little girl was blissfully unaware as a medic dressed a wound on her head.

'Ma'am,' the medic addressed Georgia.

'I'm her mother.' Georgia tore her gaze from her little girl for just a second to identify herself. 'Can she hear me?'

'She's unconscious, and I've given her a shot of morphine to keep her comfortable. She's got an open fracture to her fibula in her left leg, hence the splint. It'll need surgery to reset it. The gash to her head is superficial, but it bled a lot. She may have a concussion. We're ready to take her to the hospital.'

'Can I sit with her?' Georgia wrapped her fingers around Misty's hand.

'Ma'am, I'm sorry, but we're having to double up with patients,' the medic apologized.

'Georgia, I'll take you,' Justin said, coming to stand by her side. 'Since they merged River Springs with St. Luke's services, we're sharing the ambulances. Misty won't know you're not there.'

'*I'll* know.'

'If we go now, we'll be there before the ambulance.'

Georgia pressed her lips to her daughter's fingers. 'See you in a minute, honey. I love you.'

The medics prepared Misty for the short trip to the hospital, and Georgia let Justin guide her back to the command center to update Karen. As she buckled her seatbelt in his police car, Justin asked quietly, 'Are you okay?'

She nodded. She didn't want to talk to him; to do so would take her thoughts from her daughter, and that was all she wanted to concentrate on.

When they reached the hospital, Georgia acknowledged her thanks with a tight smile. Either Justin was incredibly perceptive, or he had just been concentrating on getting them there quickly, but he hadn't uttered another word. They entered the reception and were shown straight through to the cubicles. Georgia didn't know if Justin's job or her new status as the parent of an injured child had gotten them through the ER admission paperwork double-quick. Either way, she appreciated it.

Time passed in a blur, a sea of color and noise; doctors in white, nurses in a rainbow of scrubs, lights flashing to call for help, buzzes and beeps from medical equipment. Justin remained in Georgia's line of sight throughout; not at her side, but just there. He answered questions from concerned, even angry, parents, and talked to his counterparts by radio and phone.

Other parents arrived, greeting each other with tight hugs and kind words. There were tears and questions. The dynamics of life in River Springs unfolded before Georgia. This community came together in times of need and shared the burden with each other. She'd missed out on this growing up; her mother and father had been archaeologists and her own childhood had been spent moving from country to country, dig to dig. Georgia had loved the sense of belonging that came with being part of Justin's life, if even for a brief time. She still longed for it now, and she knew that Misty also craved a place she could truly call home. Her daughter's hopeful face from earlier that morning filled her vision. 'This might be a keeper,' Misty had said.

'It's not looking good so far, baby,' Georgia whispered.

As the other parents talked together, she felt like an invisible wall separated her from them. They had years of friendship to hold them together while their tears fell and prayers were offered. She'd keep her tears to herself. There would be plenty of time for that when she was alone.

'Parents of Misty Baxter,' a nurse called from across the hall.

Heads turned, the parents unfamiliar with the name. Georgia stood, ignoring the curious stares. She didn't know any of the other parents, but she could bet they'd heard about her. Wasn't that what happened in small towns? The bigger the grapevine, the bigger the sour grapes.

'I'm Misty's mom.'

'Come with me and I'll take you to see her,' the nurse said.

* ★ *

The little girl lay with her eyes closed, so tiny in the hospital bed. A tall older man turned with a wide and very white smile. 'Ms. Baxter? I'm Doctor Harrison. I've been assessing your daughter.'

50

He held out his hand and Georgia shook it.

'How is she?'

'She's still sedated to keep her comfortable. The paramedics at the scene treated Misty for an open fracture to her fibula — that's the thinner of the two bones in her lower leg. X-rays confirm there's also a spiral fracture of the tibia.'

'Is that bad?'

'Treatment requires traction to get the two ends of the fibula realigned, and then we'll need to stabilize the fracture of the tibia. That means surgery. We've got Misty booked in later this afternoon. Okay?'

Georgia nodded.

'Great. Nurse Cassie, please ensure Ms. Baxter completes the appropriate permission forms. We'll take care of your daughter; she's in good hands.' Another smile and the doctor left.

'Does he always talk so fast?' The consultation had taken less than a minute.

Cassie grinned. 'We call him Hurricane Harrison. He's the best orthopedic pediatrician we have.'

'What about her head?' Bandages covered Misty's hair.

'The dressings make it seem worse than it is. There's a gash above her eyebrow; it's a laceration about two inches in diameter. We've cleaned it and used butterfly stitches rather than sutures. The edges of the wound will heal better.'

'How long will she be in surgery?'

'If the traction that's on her leg now is doing its job, it should be a simple reset. They'll put a couple of pins above and below the spiral just to stop it from fracturing any further. No more than a couple of hours.'

'When will she be going down?'

Cassie consulted her paperwork. 'Surgery is scheduled in about an hour or so. You can sit with her until then.'

'Thank you.' Georgia perched on the edge of the seat.

'If you need anything, just press the

call button. I'll be at the nurses' station.'

Georgia cast a wary eye over the red button attached to the wall above the bed. She'd pressed one too many emergency buttons today; she had no intention of summoning any further officials. Justin was one official too many as it was.

As the medical team prepped Misty for surgery, Justin stopped by. 'Hey, how's she doing?' he asked.

'They're going into the OR now. They kept her sedated.'

'Best thing for her. She's going to have enough time to hurt afterward. How long's she gonna be down for?'

'The nurse said a few hours.'

'Do you want a ride to pick up your car? I'm heading back now to see how they're doing with the elevator and make sure the rest of the building stayed in one piece after we left.'

Georgia opened her mouth to respond to that, but Justin's grin stopped her retort and instead she answered, 'I should be here when she comes around.'

A nurse interrupted, 'You should go. Take a break. We'll probably keep Misty sedated for few hours after surgery and we'll bring her around slowly. She'll need you then.'

Georgia kissed her daughter goodbye as they wheeled her to the OR.

'Come on, Georgia, let's go,' Justin said. He took her by the elbow and walked her to the elevator.

She stirred herself from her thoughts about Misty and shook her head. 'I'll take the stairs.' That eyebrow again! She wondered how so much could be conveyed with that simple movement. She'd always envied Justin's eyebrow-raising skills.

'The elevator's working fine,' he told her. 'I just came up in it.'

The doors opened and he gestured for her to go in first, ever the gentleman. They entered and Georgia flattened herself against the wall, her hand clenched tightly on the rail. This elevator felt even smaller than the one at the station, especially with Justin in there too. Could a person develop claustrophobia so soon after getting trapped somewhere? Her heart had been beating fast for the past few hours, but now it took on a whole new rhythm. Her body was heating up, and she couldn't rule out that it had nothing to do with him.

They were soon out in the fresh air, and Georgia took several deep breaths. If she sat in a car with Justin, even for the few minutes it took to drive to the department, she might not have control of her actions. It wasn't like any part of her day had been within her control, and her phone was now presenting her with the next item on her agenda.

'I'm going to walk. It's not far and I need the fresh air. Thanks for the offer of a ride.' She moved away, a polite smile in place.

'Great idea. I'll walk with you.'

Georgia frowned. 'What about your

car? What if you need it to get to an emergency?'

'I've got my radio and my cell. We can take the shortcut through the park.'

Justin fell into step with her, taking long, confident strides. He swung his arms, his hands occasionally brushing her body. While he didn't seem to mind, every time he made contact she felt a skitter of electricity shoot through her. She needed to stop any thoughts about him before they started; to stop her brain from transforming the contact, the electricity, into anything that resembled a memory of all the times Justin had touched her before. Too late — she was already remembering, and she didn't want to. What could she talk about that wasn't to do with either of them? Work. That should be safe. That should be impartial.

'Do any other members of your team have apprehensions about what Sentinel can do for your department?' she asked him.

'You mean apart from Karen?'

'I mean from a work point of view. You already told me about Karen's reasons.' She didn't mean to sound quite so snippy.

'Meaning?'

'Forget it, I shouldn't have said anything.'

'Do you have a problem working with Karen?' Justin's voice took on a hard edge.

'It's not me who has the problem. I hardly know the woman.'

'There are things you don't know, Georgia.'

'And I'm sure there are things *you* don't know.'

'Our lives didn't stop after you left.'

'Neither did mine, Justin.'

'Obviously.'

'What do you mean by that?' Georgia narrowed her eyes, glaring at him.

'Let's not talk about the past. You've got a lot going on at the moment.' He jerked his thumb over his shoulder toward the hospital overlooking the park in which they stood. 'We'll get back to the department, then you can collect your stuff and get back to your daughter.'

He started to move, but Georgia wasn't finished. This conversation clearly wasn't about work, and since he'd brought it up . . . 'Why don't we just get this out the way now?' she said. 'I can do without all these veiled references to what happened.'

He snapped his head around. 'Come again?'

'What happened between us.'

'I know exactly what happened. I was there.'

'No, you weren't there. Will you please let me explain?'

'What's to explain? You left. That's what happened.' His voice was flat.

'But . . . ' She owed him an explanation, and now he didn't want it?

'No buts, Georgia. You snuck off in the middle of the night and took the coward's way out, for whatever reason. You don't get to justify your actions now, just because you think that's going

58

to make things easier for you at work.'

'That's not . . . ' Georgia's words died in her throat. He'd switched off, his attention elsewhere. They'd reached the edge of the park and were on the pavement. The police station was just down the street.

'Do your job, Georgia, then you can take your dramas back to wherever you came from. I don't need you in my life.' She heard no emotion; they were just words.

She swallowed a lump in her throat, blinked away tears, and turned to walk in the opposite direction. Frustration curled her fists. He wasn't being fair. He didn't know what had made her leave; *who* had made her leave. She hadn't wanted to go. She loved him with her whole heart. Didn't he want to know why it had all happened?

She took a step and then stopped. It wasn't right that he was putting it all on her. It wasn't right that Paul had probably been poisoning him against her all these years. Why hadn't she been stronger that night? Why hadn't she just called Justin? He'd have come to her rescue as soon as he heard the panic in her voice. He was strong. He was the only man who'd ever made her feel safe. He was hers, and she'd given him up. She had to make it right.

About to turn and make him listen, Georgia heard him whisper, 'That's right, Georgia. Walk away. Again.'

Somewhere in the distance sirens sounded. Someone else's son or daughter needed help. Georgia needed to get back to Misty. She stepped out into the road, desperate to get away. The sirens got louder. She neared the other side of the road and she could see the parking lot at the police station.

Air horns added to the blare of the sirens now. She glanced up to see a fire truck heading toward her. She could read the company name on the front, it was that close.

'Georgia!' Justin cried.

She looked at him. He was running across the road toward her. His body slammed against hers, lifting her clean off her feet, his arms wrapped around her. The momentum carried them across the pavement, slamming them to a halt against the building. Georgia felt Justin's full weight against her, winding her. His chest heaved against hers as she struggled to pull air into her lungs. His heart was pounding; her face was just inches from his. He glared at her. God, he looked as though hated her. It emanated from his narrowed eyes, the frown on his brow, and the tightness of his mouth.

'Who's going to save you next time?' he muttered, before pressing his mouth to hers in a hard, desperate kiss that stopped her breathing completely.

3

'Sweets?'

Georgia recognized the voice, the sickly pet name jarring as it echoed in her ear. She'd gone back to the park, wanting time to get herself together. Perhaps he'd go away if she kept her eyes closed.

'I thought it was you. I'd heard you were back in town.'

Georgia stood up, wanting to get away. She looked past him; he made her feel sick. 'I have nothing to say to you, Paul.'

He leaned toward her, unsteady on his feet.

'Excuse me.' She turned her head as she brushed past him, smelling alcohol on his breath.

'What, no hug for an old friend?' Paul called before she'd walked two paces. 'How long's it been?'

'Not long enough,' she muttered. He was following her, his feet shuffling. She turned to tell him to leave her alone, but he lurched toward her, arms outstretched, dopey grin on his face. He was drunk.

'You're looking good, Sweets. Sexy Sweets, that's what we used to call you,' he sniggered, like he'd told the funniest joke ever.

Georgia wrinkled her nose in distaste. She wondered if he'd just started drinking that morning or if he'd carried on from the night before. 'Goodbye,' she said firmly.

'Wait,' he barked, grabbing her wrist and pulling down so that she had to bend her knees. 'Why are you back? I thought I told you not to come back.' The grin was gone from his face and his gaze bored into her.

'It's got nothing to do with you. Let me go,' she whispered.

'You still think you're too good for me, don't you?' he slurred, leering into her face.

Georgia turned her head. The bourbon fumes were toxic. 'I *know* I'm too good for you.'

'Ha! So what did you come back for? If it's Justin, that ain't gonna happen, lady. He is over you. I made sure of that.'

'I bet you did. I heard you got booted off the force. What took them so long?' She wasn't sure it was true, but her words caught him unawares; he released her wrist. She was buoyed by his reaction and the resentment she'd harbored for this man for nine years.

'I retired on medical grounds.'

'Drink-related?'

'Stress-related.'

Georgia looked at him for a long moment. The man was a shadow of his former self. He was unkempt, unshaven, and gaunt. 'Couldn't cope with the guilt?' She wouldn't normally prod what was obviously an open wound, but he'd destroyed everything she'd had with Justin. She wanted him to take some of the pain she was feeling.

'Guilt? From breaking you and Justin up?' He ran a hand across his eyes before laughing, but it sounded weak to Georgia. 'He felt bad for a week or two, but it didn't take him long to find someone else to keep his bed warm.'

'You set him a great example to follow,' Georgia snapped.

'You're trouble,' he hissed. 'You always were. Justin doesn't need you in his life.'

'He doesn't need you in his life, either. I remember what you did to him. I remember exactly how good a friend you were to him, Paul. He would have done anything for you; anything.'

'And he still will. I'm the one who's still here. Why don't you just leave? You did it so well last time. You should remember how.'

'I remember things you probably forgot about in the bottom of a whisky bottle.' She smiled and walked backwards, heading for the department. 'I'm not going anywhere.'

'I can make things difficult for you, Sweets,' he threatened.

'Difficult? How much more difficult could my life be right now? My daughter is in the hospital; nothing could be worse than that. Goodbye, Paul.'

★　★　★

Justin knew he'd made a mistake the second Georgia kissed him back. He'd gone from holding her hand as he pulled her out of the elevator, to holding her close as the tanker exploded, and now he had her pressed against a wall, making out with her in broad daylight. All within a matter of hours. At this rate, they'd be in bed just after supper — and if that happened, he'd be the one who needed saving.

He pulled away with a growled 'No' and stupidly looked at her face before he stalked off, head low. The image of her lips was burned into his mind.

'Justin!' He heard all sorts of things

in her voice as she called after him, not least of all confusion. He rammed his hands into his pockets, fists clenched. Nine years. Nine years she'd been gone, and he'd managed fine. One day, just one damn day, and she'd managed to take him from police boss to teenaged boy, with all the mixed-up feelings that came with it.

He took a steadying breath to control the tightness in his chest before entering the department. He was a grown man; he'd dealt with harder situations than this before. But no situation had straddled the boundary between personal and professional, with feet planted more squarely on each side of the fence.

He walked across the entrance hall, heading for the stairs. His fingers closed around the door handle to his new office. He needed some time before he faced anyone.

'Boss.'

He ignored Karen and opened the door.

'Boss!' she called, and he knew he wasn't getting away that easily.

'Yeah?' He turned his head a fraction.

'Is everything okay?'

'Sure. I'll be in my office. I don't want to be disturbed. By anyone.' The door closed behind him and he took the stairs two at a time, pounding the steps, jarring his body. A ball of tightly controlled anger had moved from his chest upward, the muscles in his neck tensing. He felt as if his heart was beating in his throat.

There were only a chair and a desk in his office, and as he slammed the door the noise reverberated around the otherwise empty room. He took a seat and reached into his pocket for his cell, ready to call Sentinel and tell them to send another representative — someone other than Georgia Baxter; someone who wouldn't make him feel so damn . . . What was he feeling?

Justin's job required him to be cool and calm. Everything that had happened today was his bread and butter, the reason he loved what he did. He'd attended an emergency in the work-place and assisted at the scene of a serious traffic accident. The fact that both of them had involved Georgia in one way or another shouldn't matter, but he couldn't shake the thought that both had happened because of her. The rational part of him knew that she couldn't have caused the accident, but the irrational, emotional side was jabbing him in the chest hard, telling him that Georgia Baxter was trouble.

Didn't he know it! Had he forgotten how he'd felt when Georgia had left him, just when he needed her; wanted her the most? And he still needed her; still wanted her. What else was that kiss about in the street?

Justin groaned. He wasn't angry at Georgia. She hadn't done anything; hadn't asked to be kissed. He was angry that he was letting her get to him. Angry at himself. In fact, the more he thought about it, the more he wondered what kind of a heel he was, pinning her against a wall and kissing her when she had just left her daughter in surgery. She'd done nothing but try to explain her reasons for leaving, and he'd acted like a sulky teenager instead of the well-adjusted adult his last psych test had told him he was.

His thoughts jumped around while his foot tapped on the floor. This wasn't going to solve anything. He needed to get whatever this thing was between him and Georgia out of his system. He wouldn't be able to concentrate, let alone work with her over the coming weeks, without clearing the air.

He pushed away from his desk and out of his chair, and put his phone back in his pocket. This was just another situation he'd have to deal with professionally. If that meant drawing a mental line in the nonexistent sands of time, locking down memories and feelings from the past, then so be it. This thing with Georgia was just business, with no past and no future; just now.

He looked out of the office window

to see her walking slowly across the parking lot. *Business, Justin*, he reminded himself, trying to ignore her sagging posture. *Just business.*

* * *

Georgia entered the department and headed for the desk. A young lady was working at a computer. 'Good afternoon,' she said. 'Can I help you?'

'Yes, I'm Georgia Baxter from Sentinel. I'd just like to pick up my things from the conference room.' She forced herself to smile, matching the receptionist's pleasant greeting.

'Certainly, ma'am. We've been expecting you. I'll have someone escort you up.' She picked up the telephone and dialed.

Georgia experienced a second of panic. Was she calling Justin? The woman didn't speak to anyone, and replaced the handset. A moment later, Karen entered reception from an office to the right.

'Hi, Georgia. How's Misty?'

'She's in surgery now. I just came for my things.' She fixed a smile in place and fell in step with Karen.

'We'll take the stairs; the elevator's still out of order.' Karen opened the door to the stairwell.

'Listen, I'm sorry about this morning, Karen. I didn't mean for any of that to happen, you know.'

'It's forgotten. The company who installed the elevator say there's a known issue, and they've ordered replacement parts. Besides, who can't use a bit more exercise?' She grinned. They'd reached the first-floor landing. 'The administration team works on this floor, and the boss has an office there.' Karen indicated as they walked.

'Is he in?' Georgia told herself she only wanted to know so she could avoid him.

'He is, but he doesn't want to be disturbed. Do you need to see him?'

'No.' Georgia was firm. They reached the conference room and Georgia picked up her things.

'I thought I'd pack up for you. Will you go back to the hospital now?' Karen asked.

'I want to go home and take a quick shower. I need to take some bits in for Misty. I don't know how long she'll be in for.' Georgia's voice quavered a little, and she saw a look of empathy on the other woman's face.

'I can't imagine what you must be going through, Georgia.' Karen patted her hand on Georgia's upper arm.

'Thank you.' Georgia was comforted by her sisterly gesture. 'Do you and Paul have kids, Karen?'

Karen looked pained for a second, but the moment passed. 'No.'

Georgia's brain dredged up a memory of a tiny life that Paul had created — just not with Karen. As Karen turned away, Georgia winced. That had been an insensitive question, and from the tense set of the other woman's shoulders, Georgia knew she'd touched something raw. Her phone beeped loudly in her pocket, but she ignored it as she followed Karen down the hall.

'Aren't you going to get that?' Karen asked her.

'No.'

'It might be the hospital calling about Misty.'

'It's just my planner. I think my schedule says I should be looking at system integration in your dispatch room right about now.' Georgia gave a little laugh, hoping to lighten the mood.

They descended to the ground floor in silence, Georgia mentally kicking herself all the way. Karen must know what Georgia knew, about Paul's extramarital activity, which was why she was acting this way. Georgia's phone bleeped again, just once.

Karen stopped in the reception by the front door and leveled her gaze at Georgia. 'Life doesn't always go according to plan, and no matter how badly we want something, we don't always get things our own way.' Her voice was low, and Georgia felt a distinct chill between them.

'I'm so sorry, Karen.' Georgia was earnest as she spoke. 'I didn't mean to — '

Karen's smile was so tight, her lips turned white. 'Don't apologize, Georgia. Paul and I are happy now. It was a long time ago.'

Georgia frowned. What was it with everyone not wanting to hear her out? And that wasn't what she was apologizing for anyway. 'I'll let you know when I'll be back at work,' she said. 'It depends on what happens at the hospital.'

'I hope Misty's okay.' Karen nodded her goodbye and left Georgia standing, wondering how she'd managed to so thoroughly upset two of the people she was supposed to be working closely with.

She hadn't planned on having to deal with Karen's personal issues. At that moment in time, all she wanted to do was take her daughter home where she'd be safe, but Georgia knew it wasn't going to be that easy. Her life had gone from simple to complicated in just one day. But what else should she expect, coming back to a town where her past was waiting for her?

★ ★ ★

Georgia sat at Misty's bedside while the little girl slept. Her surgery had been successful; the broken bones were set and temporary pins in put place. Misty's leg was raised in traction, and she had come around from the anesthetic quickly, which was good. So far, the pain medication she was receiving was working.

Misty had managed a groggy smile for her mother and a hug for the favorite soft toy that Georgia had brought from home, before falling into a deep sleep. The nurse had assured her it was a primal instinct, the body's way of dealing with trauma, and to begin healing she needed to sleep.

Georgia was reading her emails, straining her eyes against the dim bedside light, when she noticed a young woman pause at the door to the room. She wore scrubs but had a casual jacket over the top.

'Hi,' Georgia said with a smile. There had recently been a shift change, and different people were now caring for Misty overnight.

'Hi. Can I come in? I'm not interrupting you?' The woman seemed unsure of herself.

'Please. I'm just checking my emails, but nothing's going in. Do you need to check on Misty?' Georgia closed her laptop and set it on the nightstand.

'I'm off duty.' She laughed nervously and indicated her scrubs as she took a few steps into the room.

'Oh, okay.' Georgia thought the woman looked familiar, but she couldn't place her. She'd seen so many hospital staff members during the day.

'You don't remember me, do you?'

Georgia stood and crossed the room.

The woman gave her a wobbly smile as she held her staff ID badge up to the light, and Georgia read her name.

'Tracy? Tracy Goodwin. Oh, my.' Georgia smiled warmly at her.

'Hi, Ms. Baxter.' Tracy giggled nervously but gladly accepted Georgia's hug.

'How are you? You look great, and you're a nurse. What happened to wanting to be a vet?' Georgia had mentored Tracy when the younger woman was a student counselor at the local high school.

'I decided I liked helping people better than animals. I can't believe this big girl is your daughter. It doesn't seem yesterday I was still in high school and you were my teacher!' Tracy moved to the bedside and looked at the sleeping child. 'I was in the ER when she first came in. I thought it was you when I saw you earlier in the waiting room, but I wasn't sure until just now. What brings you back to town?'

'I'm working at the police station,

installing software to make their processes more effective.' Georgia stood across the bed and took a good look at the woman before her. She looked so much better than the last time Georgia had seen her. Tracy had been going through a hard time in her life.

'I saw you with Detective Rose in the waiting room. I was really sorry to hear things didn't work out for you two. I used to see you both around and hope one day I'd have someone like him in my life.' Tracy smiled shyly. 'How long are you in town? It'd be good to meet up, with you and Misty.'

'I'm not sure. We move around a lot with my job, but I think Misty's getting a little tired of changing schools every six months.' Georgia paused, her thoughts rushing ahead to what only could be another crash — of the emotional kind — if she stayed in town. 'But I'm not sure River Springs is the right place for us.'

Misty stirred, wriggling as much as she could with her leg in the air, and the teddy bear she held fell onto the floor. Tracy picked it up and hugged it to her for a few seconds before tucking it back under Misty's arm. Georgia thought Tracy looked sad all of a sudden. She was reminded of the seventeen-year-old Tracy, a senior in high school, and how she had thought her life was over before it had even started.

'We can catch up now, unless you need to get home?' Georgia left the question of any family unasked; she'd learned her lesson with Karen earlier.

'Sure, I'd love to.' Tracy smiled.

'Coffee from the vending machine?' Georgia reached for her purse, but Tracy shook her head and laughed.

'That stuff is terrible. I'll go to the coffee shop; that's fresh, at least. What would you like, Ms. Baxter?'

'Georgia, please. We're not at school anymore, Tracy. I'll have a latte, thank you.'

'My pleasure.'

Tracy left the room and Georgia

moved the chair next to the camp bed that the orderlies had put in the corner. It was actually a converted gurney, and the mattress was thin, so not the most comfortable thing she'd ever slept on; but she'd do anything to be with her daughter in her time of need.

With no distractions, Georgia let her mind drift over one of the most emotional days she'd had in many years. She'd hoped to make her return to River Springs quietly. She'd anticipated that Justin would be one of the first people that she'd meet. She'd even run through how that might go. Who was she kidding? She'd thought about that day for years: imagined the conversation in her head, schooled her reaction to seeing him in person, and run through exactly what expression she would wear on her face. In all of the rehearsals, she'd never had the foresight to practice the words 'I'm stuck in an elevator' or 'my daughter's trapped in a bus that could catch on fire at any moment.'

Justin looked as good as she remembered him. Leaner, a few more lines on his face, but still a fine-looking man. Georgia couldn't remember him smiling at all today, at least not genuinely. He used to smile a lot. Maybe he didn't have much to smile about. She knew nothing about him; about his life. How had that happened? What had they talked about today? Work, Karen, how his life hadn't stopped after Georgia had left. But she knew what had happened when he pressed his body against her and kissed her, and how it had made her feel.

And she knew that he didn't want to know why she had left. Did she want to rake all of that up when he'd made himself clear? His words said one thing — that he had moved on; but his kiss told her something else. If she and Misty were to put down some roots, would her daughter be able to grow in the town where Georgia had history? She had a feeling that some of her history still had to be rewritten, and wasn't sure she liked the uncertainty of how it would pan out.

But if Justin didn't want to hear her reasons, why should she let it color the choices she made while she was in River Springs? Maybe she'd make up her mind after she'd caught up with Tracy and filled in whatever gaps she could since she'd left.

Tracy returned with two large Styrofoam cups and some Danishes in a plastic bag, which she dangled temptingly in front of Georgia's face. 'Look what I found! The coffee shop was just about to close, so I thought I'd rescue these and give them to a good home. Sorry, no latte. The coffee had been standing a while and was really strong. I put sugar in to sweeten it some.'

Georgia grinned ruefully as her stomach gurgled in appreciation. She couldn't remember the last time she'd eaten. 'Sit down. You talk, I'll eat.'

'Why do I feel like I'm back in your office at school?' Tracy teased.

Georgia shook her head. 'I think

you'll find I'm the one who needs help this time.' She pointed to Misty with the pastry she took from the bag. 'You guys have been amazing. Everyone cares so much about their patients. I'd trust you all with my daughter's life.'

'She's a beautiful little girl, Georgia. You're so lucky.' Tracy sounded wistful.

'Yes, I am. So tell me about yourself, Tracy. You stayed in town, trained to be a nurse . . . '

'I stayed in town for a few years after I graduated and took a few distance learning courses while I decided what I wanted to do. Then I studied for a bachelor's in nursing science at Columbus State. I took psychiatric care as an elective.'

'Is that your specialism now?'

'Not yet; I'm still deciding. I had had a few mental health issues after . . . well, you know, and I felt very strongly about going back. I still attend a local support group; they're there for me when life gets a bit much.'

They were silent for a time, Georgia

wary of broaching any sensitive subjects. Tracy spoke first. 'So who else have you caught up with since you got back?'

'We only got here last weekend. Apart from you and Detective Rose, just Karen.'

'Karen Denali?' Tracy paled somewhat and swallowed nervously.

Georgia nodded, unsure she'd said the right thing. After all, Tracy had slept with Karen's husband.

Tracy gave her a tight smile. 'Yeah, I see her at some of the places I go. She does a lot for Mayor Goodwin's charities too.'

'Did your daddy make mayor after all?'

'Yes!' Tracy's smile widened. 'He's been mayor for nearly four years and is hoping to get re-elected for a second term. The election is next week.'

'That's great to hear, Tracy. You must be very proud.'

'I am. The town seems to like the way he runs things. We stopped by the scene of the accident earlier. Daddy was giving me a ride into work. He's worked so hard to get to where he is.'

'As have you. I did think of you after I left. I know you were worried about how your family would react.'

For a brief moment, Tracy's face darkened. Georgia's stomach dropped. *What's wrong with me?* she asked herself. Communication skills were supposed to be her strength, but she was having great difficulty getting it right today. 'I'm sorry, Tracy. I shouldn't have mentioned anything.'

'No, don't be, please. It's strange to hear it talked about. Termination's not something that gets discussed around the dinner table, not when your daddy's shooting for re-election.'

'He doesn't know?' The elephant in the room tooted its trunk. 'Do you want to talk about it?'

'There's not much to say.' Tracy pursed her lips and wrinkled her nose. 'I went to the appointment you made for me, to talk through my options. The lady gave me a lot of information to take home and read. I was thinking about keeping the baby and started choosing names and everything. But then I started to get real bad morning sickness, missed a lot of school, got depressed. Daddy kept talking about getting me looked at, and I was scared what he'd do if he found out. So I went to the clinic and . . . '

Georgia placed her hands over Tracy's to still their nervous fluttering. 'But you're okay in yourself?'

'I have a few health issues, but nothing to stop me from getting on with my life.'

Georgia smiled. 'That's good. I admire you for picking yourself up and choosing such a worthwhile career. It must be great working in the town you grew up in and being able to help your community.'

'Yeah, you get to see the same old faces. It's a pretty small town.'

'And that's been okay, too? I mean, seeing — '

'Paul? I've seen him around a bit, but I'm not sure he even remembers sleeping with me, let alone that I was carrying his baby.'

Georgia felt an uncomfortable tug of guilt in her gut. Oh, he knew. She'd made sure of that. Paul Denali was the reason she'd left that night, and she knew what a lowlife drunk he really was.

'But you came through it.' Georgia squeezed Tracy's hand, hoping that guilt wasn't written all over her face.

'I did. I'm kind of glad I went through my wild years when I was young. I was horribly self-righteous for a while, when some of my high school friends dropped out of school or got into drugs. Paul even got kicked off the police force, and I was so happy . . . ' Tracy's voice trailed off and her thoughts were obviously somewhere else.

Of course, a police officer losing his job was common knowledge in a small town. Georgia had obviously missed a whole lot going on after she left. Was that what Justin had meant earlier? She really wanted to know what had caused his best friend to get fired from the force, but Tracy wasn't the right person to ask.

'It's been so good catching up.' Georgia waited until she had Tracy's attention and faked a yawn. 'I think I ought to get some sleep. It's been a long day.'

'Oh, I'm sorry. Sure, I'll get gone. So nice to see you, Georgia.' Tracy stood and bent to hug her. 'I hope you get a good night's sleep.'

'Goodnight.'

'Look after that little girl while I'm gone,' Tracy called softly as she left the room.

Georgia drank the lukewarm coffee quickly. It would quench her thirst until she made it to the water cooler. She crossed the room to kiss her daughter goodnight and tuck her in. It would only be another eight years until Misty was the same age as Tracy was when she became pregnant by a married man. Georgia shivered at the thought. Tracy had done well for herself, despite having some difficult choices to make; yet Georgia had seen glimpses of the frightened teenager during their conversation — and from her own lips, there were some lingering issues. Nobody went through that without having some scars, emotional or otherwise.

Georgia smothered a yawn. She really was tired, but according to her phone it was only 9:20 p.m. Just twelve hours ago she'd been stuck in that elevator, yet already it seemed like a distant memory. It was too early to go to bed, but a power nap would do her the world of good. Then she'd go and get washed and settled for the night. She glanced at the gurney with some misgiving. The chair would do for now.

* * *

'Georgia.'

She was shaking. Had the elevator

started moving again? Someone was calling her.

'Georgia.' The voice was louder, the shaking stronger. Georgia roused herself, but her eyes didn't want to open. She couldn't focus on more than the outline of a figure, who was suggesting to her she'd be more comfortable sleeping on the gurney.

'What time is it?' She was helped to her feet; her limbs felt like lead weights.

'It's quarter after ten.'

''S'early.' Two little steps and she stumbled heavily onto the bed.

'It's late,' someone said. 'Too late.'

★ ★ ★

Georgia woke to bright lights and a lot of hustle and bustle. Things got started early around here. As she swung her feet the short distance to the floor, she realized she was still wearing her shoes. In fact, she was still in her sweats from yesterday. She must have been tired.

Out in the hallway people rushed back and forth, and yet it remained quiet in the room. Georgia stretched her arms and rolled her head a few times, working out the kinks in her neck. She let her head drop backward, wincing at a jab of pain, and slowly brought her head forward. Her gaze took in the ceiling, the far wall, the mechanics for holding Misty's leg in traction, the hospital bed, the floor.

Georgia's head jerked up. No leg in traction. No Misty. She stood and crossed to the bed, placing her hands in the space where she'd last seen her child. The sheets were cold. There hadn't been a warm little body there for some time. There was still a dent in the pillow where Misty's head lay last night, but nothing else to show that she had been there.

She told herself that Misty had just been taken somewhere else for treatment, but that thought didn't want to stick in her head. It kept sliding around like butter in a skillet, dancing, skittering, until it evaporated in the heat. Her chest began to tighten, making breathing painful, and she could only take small gasps. She tried to take air in but her lungs refused to inflate. Her vision was getting dim from the edges; things were getting smaller. She knew she should do something; press the emergency button and call for someone. They'd tell her what was going on; where her daughter was.

She could hear footsteps. 'Good morning, ladies,' a nurse called out, bright and cheerful in Georgia's rapidly darkening world. Her hands still rested on the bed, but her fingers slowly clawed the sheet, handfuls of white cotton in each fist, her knuckles pale as she held on tight. Her legs were shaking, so she grabbed more, pulling the material from the tight hospital corners.

The nurse's concerned face blurred on the periphery of her vision, moving to the center, peering at her through a fisheye lens. 'Ms. Baxter, are you all right?' The nurse's voice sounded far away.

'Where's Misty?' Georgia whispered, the sheet loosening itself from the last corner as she fell to the ground. 'Where's my daughter?'

4

'Code Pink — repeat, Code Pink!'

Georgia could not move from the bed, even as the world around her moved in a blur.

'Emergency coordinator, start timing. I want this done by the book.'

'When did you last see her?'

'Check the notes. Who did the five a.m. bed check?'

'Five minutes.'

'Get security to check CCTV.'

'When did you last see her?'

'Check the staff roster. Is everybody that's expected on duty?'

'Nothing.'

'Ten minutes. Raise the alarm.'

Only fragments filtered through the haze that surrounded Georgia.

'Georgia.'

She heard Justin. What was he doing here?

'Georgia, we need to take a statement from you. Are you okay to talk to an officer?'

She turned her head. He was close. There was an intensity to his gaze this morning. 'She's gone,' she said flatly.

'And we'll find her. There was a ward check done at five this morning. Whoever took her had a two-and-a-half-hour window.'

'Took her? What do you mean, took her?' Georgia frowned. 'She's just been moved to another ward.'

'No.' Justin perched on the bed, and she slowly sat down beside him. 'The hospital staff have searched all the wards, and officers are doing a second sweep. Misty's been taken.'

'She's gone back into surgery. The operation didn't work.'

'The operation was fine. Georgia, someone's taken Misty from the hospital. She's not here.'

Panic welled in her throat, tension squeezing her voice higher. 'She got out of bed herself?' Even as she spoke, she acknowledged that it was impossible. The little girl's leg had been in traction, and the handle to wind the mechanism down was at the foot of the bed.

'This is going to be hard, and I'm afraid it'll get much worse before the end — '

'The end? What do you mean?' Georgia grabbed Justin's arm, her fingers tight.

'The end of the investigation. This is abduction, Georgia. Misty's been kidnapped.'

Georgia felt her shoulders slump. Her head dropped, she felt so weak. 'Justin, I'm scared,' she whispered as the tears began to fall. She'd kept it together yesterday, but this was too much, way too much.

As he wrapped his arms around her, Georgia's head rested on his shoulder, her face against his neck. It was wrong to feel anything other than numb, she thought, but Justin's body was solid against her; strong, warm, and safe.

Her tears wet his shirt as she quietly

wept, her body shaking, Justin took a deep breath and held her tighter. Georgia felt his lips against her forehead. They remained still for a long moment until an officer entered the room. Justin raised his head.

'We're ready to take a statement, sir.' The officer sounded unsure. 'If Ms. Baxter is ready?'

Justin could see the thoughts all over his colleague's face. Why was his boss holding the abductee's mother like that? There were some people in town who didn't know their history; but if he kept on like this that would change, no doubt about it. Georgia needed him, if only in that second. After he'd kissed her yesterday he'd sworn to keep his distance, but she needed him, and her daughter needed him too. Georgia was old news, bad news, but he had a job to do and a member of his community to help.

'Georgia, will you go with Officer Taylor to the station?' Justin stood and put some space between them, avoiding her puzzled gaze. 'Taylor, I'll meet you there after I've caught up with the hospital's security team.'

Justin waited by the window as Georgia and Taylor left the room, hoping that she didn't look over her shoulder. He was walking a very fine line between professional and personal. He couldn't afford to cross it; there was more than just his reputation at stake. There was his job and possibly his heart.

It had been a long time since any woman had made enough of a dent in his life for him to consider any kind of future with her. The last one had been Georgia, and that hadn't gone too well. The only future he could consider with her was one that involved him doing his job and finding her daughter. That had to be what he kept in his mind; just that.

Justin headed for the security office. The first few hours were the best time to find clues; to find a missing child. Standing around daydreaming about a woman who had ditched him without so much as a goodbye wasn't going to get anybody found.

★ ★ ★

When Officer Taylor questioned her, Georgia could only give a very sketchy outline of the events of the last twenty-four hours. The fact that they had been the most difficult twenty-four hours in her life was clearly not going to cut it with the police. She'd never felt so hemmed in as she did right now, in a small interview room with no windows, no air. It was more claustrophobic than the elevator yesterday.

How was asking her questions about what happened yesterday going to help to find her daughter today? The officer wanted to know if she'd had any difficult conversations yesterday with anybody. She could name two people, but as they were with his colleagues, Georgia didn't feel it necessary to go into any detail at all. She said she'd prefer to speak to Detective Rose. Officer Taylor appeared to have difficulty in accepting her answer.

'Ms. Baxter, it is essential that I get a full account of the happenings of the last few days. Vital, in fact.'

'I've been back in town for three days. Two of those I spent unpacking and setting up home. Yesterday my daughter started at a new school and I started a new job. I got stuck in the elevator here, and then my daughter was in an accident. She had surgery and spent the night in the hospital, and you know the rest.'

'Who knows you're back in town?' Taylor picked up a manila file that had lain untouched on the desk between them. He angled it so that she could read her name in bold black capital letters on the front. Great, she had a rap sheet now?

'I couldn't presume to know, Officer. After the way we arrived in your squad car, with a full complement of lights and sirens, probably everyone.'

Her sarcasm wasn't lost on the uniformed man as she returned his stare. His nostrils flared and his lips tightened. 'And does anyone here in River Springs have any cause to take your daughter?' he snapped, his eyes narrowing.

'How the hell am I supposed to know that? I doubt very many people knew I had a daughter until yesterday. Am I under suspicion?'

'I'm gathering circumstantial evidence. Doesn't it strike you as strange that your daughter is in an accident and then she goes missing?'

Georgia heard a strangled laugh — her own. 'I think this whole situation is strange. I came here to start a new job, that's all. Now my eight-year-old daughter's gone missing and you're asking me if I know who's taken her. If I knew, I'd tell you. Or are you asking me if I took my own daughter?'

'Did you?'

'Just why would I take my own child out of a hospital where she's receiving treatment for serious injuries? What kind of a mother do you think I am? Do you have children, Officer Taylor? Do you understand how it feels to see your baby in such pain? Do you?' Georgia ranted.

'It just strikes me as a coincidence that trouble happens around you and yet it's not your fault. Getting trapped in an elevator. Being at scene of an accident when you discover your daughter's involved. And then you slept while your daughter was abducted.' Taylor ignored Georgia's questions and instead threw the verbal equivalent of a gallon of gasoline onto a fire smoldering in her belly.

'How dare you . . . '

The door opened and Justin came in. 'Thank you, Taylor, I'll take it from here.' His curt tone silenced any protest from his officer. From the other side of the two-way glass, Justin didn't appreciate the way he was questioning Georgia. The man had only just been promoted and he was keen to make his mark. Justin was all for climbing the ladder; God knew it had taken him long enough to get to where he was now, especially after the investigation he and Paul had been involved in surrounding the death of two of their colleagues. His officer, however, was clearly was in need of some empathy when dealing with distressed people.

He took the seat vacated by Taylor and pushed the folder aside. 'Do you need anything, Georgia?'

'For this to all be a dream,' she replied wearily. 'Did you find anything on CCTV?'

'No one left or entered the building between five, when the last bed check was done, and six this morning. There were three deliveries between six and six-thirty. Staff began arriving between six-thirty and seven. Seven a.m. is when the night team hands over to the day shift, and then from seven onwards the doors are open to visitors.'

'What happens now?'

'We're doing a third sweep of the

hospital and going back over the tapes a minute at a time, from after the bed check. We're cross-referencing the CCTV with who clocked in and out. We're talking to the companies who made the deliveries, asking them to contact their staff, and we'll interview them.'

'You think one of them took her?'

'If I'm honest, Georgia, I don't know at this point. We've never had an abduction from a hospital in our district. All procedures are being followed to the letter.'

Justin ran his hand over his jaw and Georgia waited in silence. She didn't have that link with him anymore to be able to know what he was thinking, though his thoughts couldn't be any darker than hers. Where was her baby? What was Misty thinking right at that moment? She had to be scared. She didn't know anybody in this town, and now she'd been taken. Misty hadn't even regained consciousness after the accident so that Georgia could tell her how much she loved her; that she'd look after her; that everything would be okay.

Georgia's head bowed and her hands went to her face as an overwhelming sense of guilt washed over her. Why had she come back here? She should have known there would be trouble, though she'd never anticipated that it would involve her daughter.

'Is there any reason for someone to take Misty?' Justin's voice was soft.

Georgia shook her head, her hands sliding down her cheeks. 'Like I said to Taylor, who here even knew she existed?'

'Have any of your new neighbors shown an overt interest in you or Misty since you moved in?'

'The only person we've seen is the realtor, who met us at the house with the keys. He popped by on Sunday with his family just to say hi and to see if we wanted to join them at church.'

'Did you go?'

'No.'

'Did Misty talk to anyone that you know of? Kids in the neighborhood?'

'No. The first time she'd been by herself since we arrived is when I dropped her off at school yesterday.'

'Anyone who has a reason to get at you?'

This time she shrugged, unsure of how to answer that question without raking up the past. She wouldn't meet his gaze; he'd been doing this job for too long not to be able to read a lie. There was only one person in town she knew who might harbor any ill-feeling toward her, and he happened to be Justin's best friend. Georgia wanted to keep that little secret tucked away with the others she kept for now. It was bound to come out, but she wanted her daughter back safely first, just in case she needed to leave again.

'Okay, if it's nobody in town, tell me about your life since you left River Springs.' He looked pained for a fleeting moment, like he didn't really want to know but had to ask. Georgia remembered feeling the same way when she was younger about ripping off a Band-Aid, knowing it had to come off but that it was going to hurt.

'I don't see what this has to do with Misty's disappearance, Justin.'

'Everything. One of the things we need to establish is if this is likely to be a family abduction — whether the person who took Misty is someone connected to either of you; or if it was an opportunistic abduction. Now while I know you have no family, Georgia, I need to know if there's any reason why Misty's father or anyone known to him would want to take your daughter.'

She could answer this one truthfully, up to a point. 'I've had no contact with Misty's father or anyone to do with him.'

'For how long?'

'Since she was born.' Not a lie.

'Were you together when she was born?'

'No.' She hadn't seen him for seven

months and five days by the time Misty was born.

'When was the last time you saw him or anyone connected with him?'

Georgia mentally bit her tongue. The ice she was skating on was getting decidedly thin. 'I really don't see why I need to answer that question. I've just told you that I've had nothing to do with him since before she was born.'

'Is there a reason why you don't want to answer these questions? Is there a custody battle going on?'

'No custody battle, Justin. I can tell you unequivocally that this has nothing to do with her father. He doesn't know she exists. Can we just leave it there, please? Shouldn't you be out looking or checking something?' She crossed her arms and sat back in her chair, wanting this conversation to be over.

Whoa! Justin recognized defensive when he saw it. He could see Georgia was upset by this line of questioning, but he knew there was more. Thoughts that he'd kept suppressed because they hurt so much started to seep into his consciousness, like a suitcase too full of clothes to be zipped up; a sock sticking out here, a sleeve there. The sneaking doubt that had been kept in the dark since she left was starting to grow, and quickly. 'Do you know who Misty's father is?' He knew he was a toenail over that fine line, but he had to know.

'Of course I know who he is!' Georgia exclaimed, sitting upright and leaning forward on the desk.

Justin knew from her body language that she was telling the truth. She was opening right up, whether she wanted to or not.

'Give me his name, then. We can do a trace on him, see what his movements have been recently.'

'That won't help anyone.' She stood up with her back to him. From the rise of her shoulders, she appeared to be taking deep breaths. Justin wondered if it was nerves or anger driving her. As much as he wanted to know what she was hiding, he had played this game plenty of times before. What she was going to tell him — and she *was* going to tell him — might answer some of the questions he'd had for the last nine years, as well as help find Misty.

'You seem really reluctant to revisit your past, Georgia,' Justin said. She was tense, holding herself still, and he relaxed back in his chair. 'Whatever made you leave must still hurt bad. Do you want to talk about it? Tell me what happened?'

'You said I didn't get to justify why I walked out on you.' She turned, eyes wide, her voice shaking.

She was nervous. He was getting closer. Justin knew he was doing his job, but there was an uneasy feeling in the pit of his stomach. What if she confirmed his suspicions?

'This has to do with your time in River Springs then.' It wasn't a question and he wasn't bringing it down to the personal. It was a statement.

'I didn't say that.' Was that panic in her eyes?

'Yes you did, Georgia.'

'The fact that I left you has nothing to do with my daughter being kidnapped,' Georgia snapped, turning away, but not before Justin noticed a flush starting from her neck, moving up to her cheeks. Guilt? She didn't believe what she'd just said. She might not actually know who took Misty or why, but she had her doubts.

Justin sat silently, letting his own doubts turn into a hunch. He really hadn't planned for the conversation to take this turn, especially as it was a U-turn on what he'd said yesterday. But her reaction to his questions was taking him back in time, and he was going to have to let the painful memories free. 'I know that Paul came by the night you left.' Remembering took him back, like he was telling a story.

Georgia's shoulders slumped and Justin leaned forward.

'He said you and he got in a fight. Do you want to tell me what you fought about?'

'And you'll believe my version of events?'

Her question didn't shock him. Of course she was going to deny whatever Paul had told him. 'Try me. Tell me what happened, Georgia.'

'I don't want to do this now, Justin. I just want to find my daughter.' She turned to him, her eyes sadder than he'd ever seen.

The doubt was now in every vein in his body, seeping from every pore, and it found words. 'Then let me tell you what I know. Paul turned up drunk, looking for a friendly ear. He was devastated that he and I were being investigated.' Georgia nodded and he continued. 'You told him I was out but he could come in and join you for a drink. He didn't want to. He didn't feel comfortable being alone with you.' Her eyebrows lifted in question and Justin took a shallow breath to keep his tone neutral. 'You insisted, saying he should make himself comfortable. You said I was at work and wouldn't be home until later, much later. You poured him a drink and then you came on to him.' He could feel a vein in his temple throb; he was trying to keep his anger under control. He could hear the blood pumping in his ears. Saying it out loud, telling it the way he'd heard it from Paul a few days after she'd left, made it real. Her reactions were making it true.

'You believed him?' Georgia leaned against the two-way mirror, her hands resting on the ledge. The small gap from the desk to where she stood belied the yawning canyon that time and memory created. Was she going to deny it?

He kept his voice calm. He'd thought more of her than this. She was going to lie until she couldn't lie any more. 'What other proof did I have? You were gone. Paul was the last person to see you. What else should I have thought, Georgia? It wasn't the first time it had happened, he said.'

'No, it wasn't the first time, Justin, but it wasn't me.'

'Why would he make a pass at you? He was happily married.'

Georgia laughed, her face screwed up like she'd eaten something sour. She shook her head and Justin stared at her, willing her to look at him. Her lips thinned in a smirk. 'Make a pass at me? No, that's not what I'd call it. People keep all kinds of secrets, Justin. He wasn't that happily married,' she muttered, turning to look at the wall.

Justin took that as her admission of guilt. He waited for the usual flood of satisfaction that came after pursuing a difficult line of questioning, resulting in a confession, but it didn't come. Instead there was a slow, agonizing drip, drip, drip of bitter, dark disappointment. He hadn't wanted to believe Paul, not at the time, not in all the years since.

'Will that help you find my daughter now?'

'One more question, Georgia, then I'll have everything I need for the next stage of the investigation.' Contempt for this woman was boiling in his belly, bile rising in his throat. 'Is Paul Denali the father of your child?'

'If I tell you, I can go?' She pushed herself away from the mirror. Her head was bowed, her features shadowed as her hair fell around her face. She laid her hands flat on the table and looked directly at him. He nodded as he sat forward, his gaze holding hers.

'No, Paul Denali is not the father of my child.'

He watched her, time suspended as she reached for the door handle. The door was open and she was almost gone.

'Then who the hell is, Georgia?' He stood up sharply, the chair tumbling backwards.

Time stopped as Georgia looked Justin square in the eye. 'You don't want to know, Justin. Trust me.'

'How *can* I trust you? I don't know that a word you've told me in the last five minutes is true. Tell me the truth, Georgia.'

A look of unadulterated pain flashed across her face as she let the door close behind her, but he caught her whispered words. 'You are. You're Misty's father.'

5

Justin had no way of knowing who had witnessed his interview with Georgia. He counted to ten before he left the room, but she was already gone. He should have gone after her straight away. Better, he should have stopped her from leaving in the first place; should have realized that she would, given her penchant for running away.

How could he be so stupid, so insensitive? He had overstepped the line he'd drawn, big time. Hell, he'd set a new world pole-vaulting record.

There was no way on earth he could lead on this case if he was Misty's father. But what proof did he have other than Georgia's word? What credence could he give her claim, when she'd just lied to his face about Paul? She didn't know how hard it had been for Paul to tell Justin what had happened. How Paul had been wracked by guilt for days, coming to terms with the pain he had inadvertently caused Justin.

If there was a problem with their relationship, the first he'd known of it was when she'd left. He'd assumed such an extreme reaction was a definite admission of guilt, and in his line of work you relied on those closest to you, the ones who stayed with you, who saw you through the good times and the bad. Paul had been there for him when he'd been hauled in front of the investigation committee over the shooting of two colleagues, one of the most difficult times in his life. He relied on his fellow officers; and to have the finger pointed, to be accused of contributing to their deaths by poor management of the situation, had been almost too much to take. He trusted his team, and in turn they trusted him. He had trusted Georgia too, and relied on her to be there for him.

But she had taken that trust and all

but shoved it in his face, and now she expected him to believe that he had fathered some kid he never knew existed until yesterday. The injured child he'd carried off the bus. The little eight-year-old girl who was now missing.

Justin wished he could shake off the memory of Misty's face at the bus window. She'd been scared. What was she feeling now? How was Georgia feeling? How could he stay impartial, given his history with her? Whether he was Misty's father or not, he had to take advice from the district attorney.

On his way to his office, Taylor stopped him. The man had a furtive look about him. Justin wondered if he'd been doing some digging on Georgia and had some other big revelation to add fuel to the fire.

'Taylor?'

'Sir, I thought you might want to have this.' Taylor handed him a DVD.

'What's this?'

'A copy of the interview you held

with Ms. Baxter.' Taylor lowered his voice, even though there was no one else in the corridor.

Justin looked his officer square in the eye. 'What am I supposed to do with this?'

Would Taylor stoop so low as to try to blackmail him? Should Justin ignore him or pull him up on it? Christ, was the man that desperate to climb the ladder so quickly after being promoted?

'Destroy it, boss.'

The man looked so earnest that Justin felt like a real heel for doubting his intentions. Another black mark against Georgia. He hadn't given her more than a cursory thought for years, and now she was in his head, insinuating her way back into his life. She'd destroy his faith in humanity if he let her.

'That would be destroying evidence.'

'But sir, some of the questions you asked Ms. Baxter . . . They were . . . ' The officer let the entence trail off.

'A bit close to the mark?' Justin

grimaced as his colleague nodded. 'As were some of yours, Taylor. Thank you, but I need to speak to the DA on this matter. I appreciate the loyalty, but I've got to do this one by the book. We've got a missing child, that's what this is all about.'

Taylor nodded and stood back to let Justin pass.

A few minutes later, Justin had the DA on the phone and explained his concerns.

'Jeez, you don't do things by half.'

'Cut the wisecracks, Joe. Where do I stand?'

'In theory, there's nothing prohibiting you from investigating the case. There's no law against it, but it would certainly bring into question your findings on the grounds of bias and conflict of interest. If you take this case, Justin, you could be opening up a whole mess of trouble. Let someone else lead.'

'Thanks, Joe.'

With the decision made for him,

Justin made a call to the station to ask for an investigative officer to join him at the hospital. Then he grabbed the paperwork and glanced over it again. The formal wording on the document issued by the intelligence agencies did nothing to alleviate the niggling pain that was forming in his chest. He knew that Misty was under the age of seventeen, she was nowhere to be found, and there was reason to believe that she might be in imminent danger. If the person who had taken her wasn't aware of what the little girl had just gone through, there was a danger her injuries wouldn't heal properly.

Taylor had done his job and obtained a photograph from Georgia as well as all other critical data, such as height, weight, and hair color. Justin had an image of the girl in his mind, the way she'd looked as he carried her out the bus. What if she really was his daughter? He shook his head. He didn't have time to think about that possibility; he would deal with it when

Misty was found, safe and well.

The interview with Georgia had terminated prematurely and there was more ground that needed going over with her, but he'd happily leave that for others to do. He'd gotten more than he bargained for in their last discussion and wasn't going to take any more of her lies than he had to. He needed to keep his head and his heart straight, and focus on what was important. Raking over his past with Georgia hadn't been easy, but he had a feeling there would be more of it to come. True, Georgia didn't seem that partial to talking about it; but if Misty wasn't found soon, both of them were going to be in the frame — and Justin had already been through that once before, with fingers pointing at him following the deaths of colleagues on his watch.

*　*　*

Georgia slammed out of the building, putting as much distance between herself and Justin as possible, as quickly as she could. She didn't want to be anywhere near him. He'd accused her of having an affair, with Paul of all people. Justin had always had a blind spot when it came to his best friend. Did he really think that little of her that he'd believe she would cheat on him?

'Ugh!' she raged, stomping, her fists clenched as her arms pumped. She could feel a pulse throbbing in her temple. Justin had forced her hand — telling him he was Misty's father hadn't featured on her agenda while she was in town, but he'd put it right at the top. He had that way about him still, able to get the truth out of her. He'd been like that when they were together: he could tell that she'd had a bad day at work, or if she had concerns about a student. He'd work on her until she spilled the beans, and then he tried to make things better.

Of course, he was like that in his professional life too. That was his job: to extricate fact from fiction, right from wrong. But in truth, she was angrier with herself right now than with Justin. Had she really thought that coming back to River Springs was a good idea? That she could just carry on with her life without anyone wanting to know about her daughter; about her life since she'd left? She knew what a small town was like. News travelled fast.

She also knew that people had secrets. She had her own still, despite the biggest of these now being right out there — and with the one person she hadn't wanted to know. Justin wasn't going to let this go, but she didn't have the time to worry about him. All of her energy had to go into finding her daughter.

She was glad she hadn't seen the look on his face when she spoke those words. Probably he wouldn't believe that either; but to actually ask her if that sleaze was Misty's dad — where had that come from? What other lies had Paul been spreading in her absence?

Georgia's chest hurt as she realized she had reached the park, her lungs crying out for air. She let go of the breath she'd been holding in, forced her muscles to relax, and slowed her pace. Tense didn't even begin to cover the stiffness in her body. She took a seat on the next bench, closed her eyes, and took deep breaths.

You're going to have to deal with it sooner or later. She took another breath and forced the words from her head. *Misty, Misty, Misty,* she chanted silently.

He's not going to go away, you know. He's going to want answers now, no matter what he thinks. It's human nature. He thinks you were unfaithful with his best friend. What does that do to a man, thinking that for nine years, with no one to tell him any different? Justin knows you weren't telling him the whole story. He's a cop; that's his job.

Georgia stared at the inside of her eyelids, taking a deliberate breath.

That's enough, she told herself. *No more Justin. No more Paul. Just Misty.*

★ ★ ★

At the hospital Georgia headed to the pediatric ward, using the stairs. There were a few officers in reception, but no one challenged her. If she could just be alone in Misty's room and curl up on the bed for a little while, just to feel close to her . . . As she walked down the hall, she half-expected to see a police cordon and an armed guard, but there was neither.

She paused just outside the door, taking a breath and preparing herself for the emptiness that would ensue; the reality that her precious girl was missing. It had been just two hours since she'd awoke to find her gone; two hours in which her world had disintegrated around her.

Entering the room, she focused on the bed. There was a blonde-haired girl asleep, and a woman resting her arms and head on the mattress as she sat at the bedside.

'Misty,' Georgia gasped and rushed to the bedside. The girl didn't respond.

The woman raised her head. 'Can I help you?'

'You found her. Where was she? Is she okay?'

'I'm sorry, I don't understand.'

'My daughter! Oh, Misty. Mommy's here.'

'This is my daughter. I'm sorry, I don't know what's happened to yours, but this is Kristen.' The woman stood, pressing the call button as she did so.

A nurse entered the room. 'Is everything okay, Mrs. Talbot? Hi, Kristy. How are you feeling?' The nurse beamed, looking between the child and the two women.

Georgia took a step back. 'Why are you in my daughter's room?' She looked accusingly at the woman and the nurse. 'This is my daughter's room. She'll need it when she comes back.' Her voice rose an octave.

'I don't think — ' the nurse began.

Georgia turned on her. 'Why would you do that? Why have you given Misty's room to someone else? You should keep it for her until she comes back. They're looking for her right now. It won't be long, and then you'll have to move this girl somewhere else.'

'The room wasn't being used.' The young nurse reddened, flustered at Georgia's aggression.

'It was up until this morning!' Georgia shouted, like it was the nurse's fault. 'You were supposed to look after her. You were supposed to keep her safe. How could you let this happen?'

The little girl started to sob, and her mother shouted at the nurse to get the crazy woman out. Above it all, Georgia could hear someone screaming, a tirade of sounds; nothing was making sense. The noise was too much. She covered her ears and felt her cheeks stretching. Why was her mouth open?

Justin appeared in front of her. He was talking to her, but she couldn't hear him above the wailing. The person was in pain; that was how it sounded. He tugged her hands from her ears and she registered a growing ache in her jaw. She met Justin's gaze and then reeled as he yelled her name at the top of his voice.

The screaming stopped.

Justin and another man escorted Georgia to the administration offices and into another small room. She was crying and couldn't stop, the sobs wracking her body. She brushed away one tear only for it to be replaced with two more. She needed to breathe. She clamped her lips together to stop the sobs, and gradually she felt able to.

Justin sat beside her and introduced the other man as Officer Cross. She nodded her head in acknowledgement; she didn't trust herself to speak.

'Ma'am, I wanted to update you on what's been happening since your daughter was reported missing. You know that we've searched the hospital and been in contact with the staff and volunteers who were here during the timeframe that Misty was abducted. They've all been interviewed. We're also in the process of talking to the drivers who made deliveries this morning. Because of the circumstances of this abduction, the Georgia Bureau of Investigation has issued a Levi's Call. It's our version of the Amber alert. What this means is that your daughter's details have been given to all law enforcement services across the state, and also entered into the national crime system.' Cross spoke calmly, politely ignoring Georgia's sniffles and hiccups as her tears slowed and then ceased. 'Do you understand all of that, ma'am?'

'Yes, sir.'

'We'll have to perform a search of your home. Will you be willing for that to happen, or would you rather I obtained a warrant from the judge?'

'No, you don't need a warrant. I have nothing to hide. I just want you to find my daughter.'

'We'll also search the school. Is there

anywhere else you've been with your daughter since you arrived in River Springs on . . . ' Cross looked at the manila file Georgia recognized from her earlier interview. ' . . . Saturday?'

'We stopped by the grocery store on our way to the house on Saturday, but we didn't leave the house until Monday morning, when I took Misty to school. We were trying to get the place straight. I wanted to get settled in.' It seemed like a lifetime ago.

'Okay. Now, I believe you've already spoken to Detective Rose about possible suspects. Do you have anything to add at this point in time?'

'No, sir.'

A knowing look passed between the two men and Georgia wondered what they weren't telling her. Why was Cross doing all the talking? Wasn't Justin supposed to be in charge?

'We'll need to talk to you again after we've made our searches. Are you happy for us to go now? Do you have a spare key we can use?'

'I've only got one set. I planned on getting some cut but I didn't have time.' She opened her purse to retrieve the keys, emptying the contents onto the desk. 'I'm sorry, I can never find anything. Here you go.'

'Thank you, ma'am,' Cross said. 'We'll be as quick as we can. I'll let you know when we're done.'

'I'll see you out,' said Justin. 'Wait here, Georgia,' he instructed her, but Georgia was too busy digging in her purse looking for tissues and didn't see the men leave. She came across a photo of Misty on her last day at her previous school, before they'd moved. The girl was dressed in her favorite outfit with a huge, gappy smile on her face; she'd just lost another tooth. It had been loose for a few weeks and she'd been so happy when it had come out, laughing that the tooth fairy would have to pay out big this time. Tears came again, plopping onto the glossy paper, and Georgia scrubbed them away. She had to be strong.

Justin returned quickly and asked, 'Have you eaten at all this morning?'

'No.' She hadn't given food a thought; but now he'd mentioned it, her stomach growled.

'Let's grab a bite in the restaurant. It's still early so we shouldn't be disturbed.'

They walked in silence together, Georgia still clutching the photo. Justin ordered omelets and coffee for them both. It felt wrong that she could be doing something so ordinary, so routine, while her daughter was who knew where with some stranger.

Justin drained his coffee and Georgia wondered if he had to go, but instead he leaned forward, his arms resting on the table. 'Georgia, about what you told me earlier. About being Misty's father.' Georgia waited to see what was coming. 'Whether it's true or not — '

'I didn't lie to you,' Georgia interrupted, but he raised both his hands to stop her.

'Whether it's true or not, it changes things.'

'Between us?'

'No, not between us. This isn't about us. But it changes things on the case. If there's even the slightest chance I am her father, I can't investigate in any official capacity.'

'What do you mean?' He had to be involved; she trusted him, even if he didn't trust her. A pulse started in her neck, her muscles tensing. 'You said you'd find her. Why can't you work the case?'

'It's a conflict of interests.'

Georgia tried to process the information. Horrible images were flashing through her mind. 'Please — I trust you. Why can't you help?'

'I didn't say I wouldn't help you. I just can't do anything in an official capacity. If it ends up going to court, the prosecution could rip any evidence I put forward to shreds. Please understand, Georgia. That's why I handed the case over to Cross. He can run this investigation with a complete lack of bias.'

'So could you, Justin. You don't know Misty. You've never even met her, not properly.'

'I have, as it happens. I spoke to her when I brought her in from the bus.'

'You? You rescued her?'

Justin nodded. 'We chatted some. She told me her leg hurt. But that's not the reason. Officially, if I wanted to — if I was still on the case — I could use every resource the state has to find her, beyond prejudice.'

'Then do it. If I ever meant anything to you, Justin, please help me.'

'I'd risk losing my job, Georgia. I can't go through that again. I've worked hard to get to where I am. I can't risk it.'

'She's your daughter!'

'According to you.'

'You don't care. No one cares. No one wants to help.'

'That's not fair, Georgia. You need to believe in the system and trust that the police will do everything they can to find Misty.'

'I trust you, Justin, but not the system. Even if you don't believe me about Misty, I trust you. I know you. I don't know these people. Why should they help me?'

'Because it's their job. You've got to have faith in the relationship, and you've got to be honest. That's the only way it'll work. You've got to be open.'

'How do you know all this? Have you worked on an abduction case before?' Georgia was desperate for reassurance.

'No, but it's the same for any case where you work with the family. You get close; you get to know them. Some cases go on for months.'

Georgia sat quietly for a few minutes, taking on board everything she'd heard. 'I can't do this on my own.'

'You don't have to.'

'I don't know what I'm supposed to do. I don't know anything.'

'The sheriff's office will guide you through everything you need to do. I don't know what help I can give, apart from supporting you, Georgia.'

'Should I be out looking? Where do I start?'

'You can start by being honest with me. Is there anyone in your life who'd want to hurt Misty? Anyone you've been involved with in the last few years, who might have something against you?'

'No, I told you. There hasn't been anyone. We never stayed anywhere long enough to make deep friendships, either of us. We've just moved clear across the country. Who would want to follow me here?'

Justin looked pained. 'Then it has to be someone here in River Springs.' Georgia shrugged. 'A high percentage of child abductions are by someone known either to the victim or their family. There has to be something, Georgia. Remind me again who you've been in touch with since you've been back; people who knew you before.'

'The only people that I've had any

sensible conversation with are you, Karen, and Tracy.'

'Tracy — she's a nurse, right? Was she on the night shift?'

'No, she finished work last night and stopped by to see me on the way home.'

'What did you talk about?'

Georgia began to feel hemmed in, even though they were in a public place. 'We just caught up and talked about her work.' Justin was watching her closely and she didn't like his scrutiny.

'You and Karen were frosty toward each other yesterday.'

'She's bound to be protective of a newbie coming in and telling her how she can do her job more efficiently.'

'Is that all it is?'

'Justin, what are you getting at?' She shifted uncomfortably in her seat, sitting back and removing her hands from his.

'I'm just trying to get a feel for the relationships you have with people.' He signaled to the waitress for more drinks.

'I don't remember you being great friends with Karen when we were together.'

'I wasn't. I only met her a handful of times, when I moved in with you. You mentioned she was angry with me for walking out on you. Is that because of your friendship with Paul, or because of her relationship with you?' She was being petty, trying to get back at him for thinking she'd slept with Paul.

'I'd imagine because she saw how lost I was when you left. When I needed you most, with the investigation going on at work, you deserted me.'

Georgia pursed her lips, not about to get drawn into it. She'd only say something that was bound to come back and bite her in the backside later. 'Well, I guess that all worked out all right, since you made boss.'

'It took a lot longer than I'd hoped. Even though the investigation found no one responsible and the coroner decided accidental death, that kind of thing has a way of clouding everyone's opinion of a person.'

'And how did Paul come out of it? Unscathed, no doubt.'

'What's it to you?'

'Nothing. He just has a way of snaking his way out of everything.'

'Have you seen him?'

'Yes.' She remained tight-lipped.

'When?'

'Yesterday, right after you — '

'After I what?'

'After you kissed me. I went to the park. He was drunk.'

'What did he say?'

'Not a lot.'

'And you had no words of welcome for him after nine years?'

'That'd mean I'd have to miss him. I didn't. Ever.'

'He must've said something.'

'He slurred, if you must know, mostly crap. It doesn't matter. It's not important.'

'How do you know it's not important?'

'Okay then, *he's* not important.'

'Then if it's of no consequence, why won't you tell me about it, whatever it is?'

Georgia stood and walked to the window, looking out over the green grass, a pleasant area for patients and visitors to be in the open air. 'Is it really going to help the investigation? You just told me you're not on the case anymore, Justin. I can't think of a single reason why it'd make any difference.' She hugged herself tightly, her voice low. 'Unless this is about getting back at me for leaving you?' She didn't want to look at him. It would be there in his eyes — the accusation; the fact that she'd hurt him. 'You've handed the case over,' she continued. 'You were my anchor in this. But if you can't investigate, you've as good as cut me adrift. I don't know anyone else in this town who can help.'

Justin joined her at the window. 'Then know that I want to help you. If I ever meant anything to you, Georgia, tell me what's holding you back.'

'I don't see how what happened nine years has anything to do with today. No one here's ever met my daughter. There's no point in unraveling history. What happened, happened, and despite my worst fears it looks like everyone came out of it okay.'

'I have no idea what you're talking about. You're not making any sense. What made you leave?' He ran his fingers through his hair, an exasperated sigh escaping him. 'If I'm Misty's father, then you're going to have to open up to me.'

'I can't. No good will come of it.'

'Don't you want to find her? Your daughter's missing. Our daughter. I have a say in this, don't I, Georgia? You told me I'm her father. Doesn't she deserve a chance to have two parents instead of one? Or are you going to carry on being selfish and deprive her of a chance to know her dad? I know that you didn't love me, but don't you love her?'

'I loved you.' Georgia's words were

fierce, as she turned to face him. 'And of course I love her.' Then she slumped her shoulders, defeated. 'You'll hate me, even more than you do already.'

'That's up to me, isn't it?'

His harsh retort made her wince. 'It'll ruin everything,' she whispered.

'You already ruined everything when you left me. You kept my daughter from me.' He grabbed her shoulders and pulled her close to him, his face inches from hers. 'Tell me. Everything. You owe me that.'

6

Georgia could see he was angry, and it was genuine. This was the reaction she'd expected to get on their first meeting, but he'd clearly held himself in check. Could she get away with glossing over the worst of it? His eyes narrowed, his fingers tightening on her flesh. No, this was the time to give it up. It wasn't going to help them find Misty, but she owed Justin the truth. He needed to know why she'd left and what sort of person Paul really was. But would he believe her?

'Okay,' she said quietly, aware of other customers entering the restaurant, 'I'll tell you. But not here. It won't be easy for me to do, and it won't be easy for you to hear.'

Justin nodded. 'I'll see you out there in a few minutes. I just need to let the station know where I am,' he said curtly, and stalked out.

Georgia let a breath go and retrieved her purse. She felt so tired. Her limbs were heavy, and the weight on her shoulders was only going to increase. Slowly she wandered outside, heading for the lake. How much should she tell Justin? Should she share Tracy's story with him?

Lost in her memories, she didn't hear Justin approach from behind. 'Cross and his team are at your house now,' he said. 'They're conducting their search. He said most of your stuff is still in boxes.' She nodded. 'They're going to have to get everything out.'

'Saves me a job.' Her lighthearted quip landed with a thump on the ground, if the muscle pulsing in Justin's temple was any clue.

'Do you want to sit?' He pointed to a nearby seat.

'No, I'd rather walk.' She didn't add that she could run away more easily if he didn't like what she had to say. Run away? That was what she always did.

Ever since her parents had died, she'd never settled. The first and only time she'd been anywhere near it was with Justin — but Paul had put paid to that. And so she'd kept on running. But she couldn't run now, not with Misty gone.

They walked around the lake twice before she spoke. 'I don't know where to start.'

'At the beginning?'

'There was no beginning, really. It just happened.'

He stiffened. She knew where his thoughts lay. 'Justin, I never cheated on you. Not with Paul, not with anyone. I wouldn't have hurt you for the world. But fate was against me that night.'

'Cut the crap, Georgia. I don't believe in fate. If fate had any sense, if *you'd* had any sense, you'd have never have come back here. But you did — you made that choice, and now we've got to deal with what's happening. Leave emotion out of it. Stick to the facts,' he snapped. 'I'm a grown man. You don't have to spare my feelings.'

'Okay, facts it is.' But her heart contracted.

Without emotion, without sharing her feelings about what she'd gone through, there was no way Justin would believe what she had to say. While she dealt with plain facts and figures in her professional life, her personal life was a patchwork of color and emotion where plain old black and white were the wrong shape to fit.

'Paul came over that night — drunk, as usual. He said he knew you were at work. He wanted to come in, but I didn't want him to. I told him I was going to have an early night and he said he'd be happy to join me. He pushed past me anyway, and started talking about how he was jealous of what you and I had, and how Karen was always on his back. He said it wasn't fair that good things always happened to you; that you were going to make boss one day while he'd just stay a grunt.'

'Why would he feel that way? I was the same rank as him. We always did everything together. He's like my brother.'

Georgia shrugged. 'He wanted what you had, and apparently that meant me. He cornered me in the kitchen, pinned me against the fridge, and tried to kiss me.' She glanced at Justin but his face was impassive. 'I told him no, to leave me alone, but he kept trying. He's a big man; he was strong. Nothing I said made any difference.'

They walked in silence. Justin bent his head, his shoulders bowed, and Georgia knew he'd retreated into himself.

'I told him to back off; that I knew that he'd cheated on Karen.'

'Yeah? And where did you hear that?'

'From the person he slept with. He got her pregnant. He just laughed at me and said I could add that to the list of people he'd betrayed; it wouldn't make any difference. I didn't know what he meant, so he told me.'

'What did he tell you?'

Georgia ignored his question; that

particular subject could wait. If Justin didn't believe her about his best friend's sleazy come-on, he wasn't going to swallow another betrayal by Paul. 'I asked him how he could live with himself, and he kept laughing. He said it didn't matter, because it was all going to be fine. Then he started to . . . ' Georgia stopped at the look of total disbelief on Justin's face. He would want proof, evidence, and she knew her explanation sounded weak and contrived.

'What?' he said.

'He dragged me into the bedroom and threw me on the bed. He told me that I was going to have sex with him. He couldn't see why I was so special, but I must be if I kept you happy in bed.' She shivered. The memory was one she preferred not to think about. She was silent, pulling the sleeves of her sweatshirt over her hands.

Paul had been in her space that evening and had occupied space in her head ever since. Just the thought of him actually doing what he said he wanted to made her feel sick.

'He said the two of you did everything else together, so why shouldn't he have me too. When I said I was going to tell Karen about what he was doing to me, he told me to try it and see what she'd say. I said I'd tell you — tell you everything.' She paused, her hand going to her throat. 'He grabbed my neck. I couldn't move. He kept pressing harder, and I couldn't breathe.' Her breath caught in her throat at the memory.

Justin stopped walking and touched her arm. 'He attacked you? He raped you?'

'He was so blind drunk, he ended up passing out before . . . before he could . . . But he kept saying that you were brothers; that you'd take his side every time.'

'Do you really think that?' His question was earnest but his expression was sad, like he was upset that she didn't think he'd believe her.

'I didn't know what to think, Justin. He said that you'd be there for him, no matter what. That it wouldn't matter what I said; you'd always have his back, no matter what he did. He said if I loved you I'd leave, because if he was going down, you were going with him.'

'What did he mean by that?'

She ignored the question again. She had to stop giving him clues. She didn't mean to; it was just all tied up together, all of Paul's lies and backstabbing. If Justin hadn't found out over the last nine years, there really wasn't any point in him knowing now. Paul had been here with him; she hadn't.

'Georgia, I don't understand. It doesn't make sense. You left me because of a drunken threat from a man who attacked you? What did he mean, he was going down?'

'I'm sorry, Justin.' She looked into his eyes, his confusion evident, then began to back away. She'd all but put the gun in Paul's hand, but she'd be damned if she'd be the bad guy and pull the trigger. 'You asked for facts. If you want the how and why, you'll have to ask Paul.'

* * *

Justin stopped by Paul's office. His secretary said he hadn't been into work yet.

'Where is he, Alison? The usual?'

'Yes. He hasn't done any work since Monday. He came in this morning wearing the same clothes he had on yesterday. I told him to go home and clean up; he wasn't needed here. There's nothing for him to do. Things are real slow.' Alison had known them since they were young and took a motherly interest. She looked at Justin over her glasses. 'You should stop by more often. I think he could do with a friend. I get the impression things aren't going so well at home.'

'A friend, huh? I'll go visit with him now.' He opened the door, calling his thanks as he left.

It took him just twenty steps to reach the bar that was Paul's second office. The bar owner looked up as he entered. 'Boss.' This wasn't the first time Justin had been in looking for his buddy. 'He's in the booth. Can I get you anything?'

'A cup of coffee would be good, Charlie, thanks.'

Paul was slumped against the wall, legs sprawled across the bench. Justin slapped his feet to the floor so that he could sit.

'Lookee here, if it isn't Rose. To what do I owe this pleasure?' Paul drawled, neck-high in whisky, and all before noon.

'You got some sorrows to drown, P? You been keeping yourself busy, apart from drinking?'

'Don't you start. You sound like Karen, bro. Can't a man enjoy a quiet drink every now and then?' He lifted the drink in his hand, draining the last drops of alcohol, one eye closed as he examined the empty glass. 'Charlie, man, another over here,' he called, waving his arm wildly in the air. The bartender caught Justin's eye as he delivered his coffee, and Justin gave an imperceptible shake of his head.

'I think you've had enough for now, P.' Justin grabbed his wrist and removed the glass, banging it on the table. Paul jumped as if he'd been taken by surprise.

He was a mess. Justin found it hard to look at him. Paul was big and strong, his reactions usually lightning-quick. Back in the day, when they were rookies together, if anyone had grabbed his hand like that they'd have been up against the wall in an arm lock quicker than you could blink. Paul held the record at the academy for quick-draw on the shooting range; he could fire off shots quicker than anyone in their class.

They'd all liked a drink in the early days of joining the force — a chance to unwind with your buddies; forget the stress of the day. But Justin had found other ways to cope, especially after they'd lost two of their team. He'd had

Georgia to go home to. After Internal Affairs had finished their investigation, Paul seemed to go downhill, off sick with stress more often than he was at work. As Justin had climbed the ranks, Paul had stayed still, desk-bound until he was retired due to ill health. That was the official line, anyway — but Justin had his doubts.

'Lighten up. Anyone would think your world had ended,' Paul laughed, clapping a hand on his friend's shoulder. 'Hey, or is it just that bitch showing up again that's gotten you so serious?'

Justin shrugged him off. 'I take it you mean Georgia. How do you know she's back?'

'I'm a private detective, ain't I?'

'Is that what made you go on a bender, Georgia coming back? Because the way I heard it, you've been drinking since yesterday.'

'What?' Paul supported his head with one hand, his elbow sliding across the table as he leaned heavily. 'Why would I care about her? She never did anything for me. I couldn't care less if I never saw her again.' His hand slid upwards, pulling his mouth sideways in a leer, his cheek squashing his eye all but closed. 'The question is, bro, do you care? Is she getting you hot, even after all these years? I never saw the attraction myself.'

'Georgia and I had a long chat about why she left.' Justin kept his tone steady. He was angry at Paul for getting in this state, but needed to keep him calm, to hear what he had to say about Georgia's claim.

'Yeah? What bullshit did she come up with?' His head lolled as if he was falling asleep but he lifted it, looking at Justin, his eyes bloodshot. He coughed, spluttering saliva. 'Let me guess. She's still in love with you, and she's been pining away for however many years. She had to come and see if you'd give her one last chance. Go on, tell me, what did she say?'

'That you attacked her the night she left.'

'Ha, she said that?' Paul grinned. 'More like the other way around. She was up for it, dressed up in those skimpy little shorts and tank top.' He ran a furry tongue across his lips lecherously. 'She asked me in and offered me a drink. She couldn't wait for me to — '

'She said you got some girl pregnant,' Justin interrupted, not waiting to hear what came next. 'Did you cheat on Karen?'

Paul frowned as if he was trying to understand. 'I can't get my own wife pregnant. How am I supposed to get anyone else pregnant? What the hell has that got to do with you?'

'Are you denying it?'

'No one's ever given birth to my child, Justin, if that's what you're asking. There's no Denali Junior anywhere on this planet. Not for want of trying.' He lifted his head, his glassy stare focused for just a split second.

'What happened with you and Georgia that night? I need to know,

Paul. It's important.'

'Hell, I don't even remember what happened two nights ago, let alone nine years ago. She left; you moved on. Why's it so important?' He folded his arms and rested his forehead on them.

'Her daughter was abducted. I'm looking for clues from her past.'

'And you think I've got something to do with it?' he mumbled against his sleeve. 'What mug did she get to father a kid? Don't tell me, she's blaming me!' He began to snigger.

'No; she says I'm the father.'

The snigger turned to a snort. Justin met Paul's gaze as he turned a baleful eye toward him. 'You?'

'Yeah, me.'

'Can she prove it?'

'You're the private investigator. What do you think?' Justin frowned. His friend seemed suddenly much more alert.

'It's not like you can do a DNA test if the girl's missing. She could be pulling a fast one. Have you asked for a birth certificate?'

'I only found out a few hours ago.'

'When?' Paul sat up.

'When what?'

'When did she tell you? What were you doing?'

'I was interviewing her. I was trying to ascertain if the kid's father would have any reason to take her.'

'And she just came out and said it?'

'No.' The question made Justin feel uncomfortable. 'No, I asked her if she knew who the father was. Then I asked her if you were the father.'

'Me?' Paul stared incredulously.

'Is there any chance?' Justin really wanted this conversation to be over. He didn't like the way his friend was reacting. Had Georgia told the whole truth? She might have held something back, for fear of . . . fear of what?

'Bro, she told you that to get you to help her, to get you on her side. Who's going to try harder to find the daughter but her father? She's playing you, man, messing with your emotions.' Paul sat back, like he'd solved the whole mystery.

'But I'm not on the case, not anymore, not since she told me that. I spoke to the DA and he advised me to remove myself. Better all around.'

'Who's taken the case? Taylor?'

'No, sheriff's office and GBI are aware. I talked with both and a Levi's Call has been issued. It's gone state-wide.'

Was it the light in the bar, or had Paul gone pale? Justin watched him swallow.

'That's some serious shit, man.'

'You look worried, P.'

'I need to be sick,' Paul mumbled, struggling to get out of the stall before heading for the men's room.

How much had he drunk? Georgia had mentioned seeing Paul on Monday afternoon and he'd been drunk then. Justin wondered what had tipped him over the edge. Was business so good that he could afford to go on a binge?

Or were things so bad that he was drinking to forget? Alison said things were real slow earlier. Something was up with Paul, whether professionally or personally.

Paul returned via the bar, asking Charlie for a glass of water. He got a jug. 'Sorry, Justin. That last shot of bourbon tipped it,' he said after downing two glasses of water.

'Is everything okay?'

'Business is slow, but we're in a recession, right?' Paul smiled, but it didn't make it to his eyes. 'Karen had her birthday last weekend.'

'Hey, I'm sorry, I forgot. Did you celebrate?'

'Don't sweat it. I forgot too.'

'Oh, man.'

'Yeah, right. I tried to make it up to her, you know.' Paul gave him a lecherous grin. 'But she was upset with me — uptight that she's getting older; angry that she doesn't have kids.'

Justin opened his mouth to offer his condolences, as he had done many times before. Karen had never made any secret of her desire to start a family; it had just never happened for them. His friend held his hand up to stop him.

'Save it. We both know she goes through these phases. I've offered to remortgage the house to get IVF treatment, but she says it's not natural. It's almost like she'd be admitting defeat if she tried to have a baby any other way. We even talked about adopting, but she says it's not the same. I think every now and then it gets to her. She came to the office on her lunch break on Monday, upset by the school bus incident, and caught me drinking. She accused me of not caring, and she stormed out. When I got home the arguing picked up where it'd left off. She was real angry that Georgia had come back to town and after two days her daughter had been hurt in the accident.'

'Why should that bother her?'

'I asked her the same thing. She

yelled that some people were just careless with their children and didn't deserve to have them. Then she kicked me out and told me not to bother coming back. I checked into the motel yesterday afternoon.'

'Have you spoken to her today?' Justin hadn't seen Karen at work that morning.

'She's sick in bed with a migraine. I only know that because I snuck in this morning to get a change of clothes. Alison sent me packing from the office, telling me I was a disgrace and I oughta be ashamed of myself.'

'I can imagine.' Justin grinned.

'She screamed at me from the top of the stairs, throwing shoes at me, telling me to get out, to leave her alone. She needed space; had to figure things out.' Paul rubbed his eyes.

'Looks like you could do with some shuteye. You know, you could have stayed at mine last night. *Mi casa, su casa.*'

'Thanks, man, but by closing time I

didn't know my own name. Charlie said he practically carried me over the road to the motel and dropped me off in the reception. It's not the first time.' He grinned, showing no shame. 'Besides, if this whole daddy thing works out, you might be needing that guest room.'

'Let's not go there. That's a long ways down the road. We've got to find her yet.'

Justin couldn't entertain the notion of being a daddy. There was too much present, and apparently a whole heap of past, to get through before he could think about the future. They didn't have any clues to go on. None. Plus he was off the case, and it was only out of professional courtesy that the sheriff's office had kept him up to date thus far. There was no reason other than Georgia's say-so that he had any right to be involved in this case as a relative, but he couldn't take a chance and get involved in the investigation.

To get an outcome in a court of law, where proof was essential to get a conviction, hard facts and physical evidence were the only way to ensure justice was served. To get there, however, hunches had to be followed; theories had to be tested to get to that truth. Justin was relying on his gut to get him through the emotional minefield to reach Georgia. His insides would knot up if he let thoughts of Misty somewhere cold and dark enter his head. Again, there was nothing to suggest that she was being held in such conditions, but there was nothing to suggest she wasn't. He had to get his head straight. He was no good to anybody if he couldn't remain neutral. *He* needed help if he was going to help Georgia.

'Paul, would you be able to do some digging for me?'

His question seemed to snap Paul out of a daydream. What had he been thinking about? Karen, or his next drink? Whatever it was, it took a few seconds for his eyes to focus.

'Now?'

'When you've sobered up. Can you find out about a nurse called Tracy Goodwin?'

'The mayor's daughter?' Paul looked surprised, but the expression was gone before Justin could comment.

'You know her?'

'Karen sometimes talks about her. She knows her from the mayor's fundraisers and the hospital. What's she got to do with all this?'

'Maybe nothing. But apart from you, me, and Karen, this Tracy's the only other person Georgia's spoken with since she got here. She was on shift on Monday, and stopped by Misty's room to catch up. Tracy was a student at the high school when Georgia worked there.'

'Okay, I'll see what I can find out.' Paul took his phone out of his pocket and set a reminder, then took a long look at Justin. 'Why go to all this effort if you're not on the case, Justin? You don't owe Georgia anything and you never met this little girl.'

Justin blinked away Misty's face. 'I rescued her from the bus yesterday.'

'You did?'

Justin swallowed back a lump of emotion.

'Do not get attached, Rose. There's nothing tying you to her.'

'I was just helping the firefighters out.'

Paul nodded, still looking closely at his friend.

'I'd better get going. I've got a station to run.' Justin stood. 'Let me know if you find anything.'

'I will. I'll get cleaned up, have lunch, and head into the office.'

'Appreciate it.' Justin turned to leave and then thought better of it. 'Georgia mentioned something else you said — about taking me down with you.' He looked closely at Paul, waiting for his reaction. 'What did you mean?'

'Bro, why would I say something like that?'

Justin looked at him, allowing the silence to stretch. Paul gave him a tight smile, standing a little unsteady on his feet. 'I'd take everything she says with a bucketful of salt, Justin, because she's rubbing it in deep. Be careful.'

7

Georgia needed relief, pain relief in the first instance. It felt like great big lumps of blood were coagulating inside her body. She was sure that clots were squeezing through the tiny vessels in her temples and behind her eyes, such was the throbbing pressure of her headache. A foraging expedition into her purse hadn't turned up any medication, and the hospital pharmacy did not sell any over-the-counter tablets. An orderly had pointed her in the direction of the grocery store, where there was a drug counter, and that was where she was headed, slowly but surely treading the familiar pavements of what constituted downtown River Springs — all three streets of it.

She passed a bar and wondered whether she would get the kind of numbness she was hoping for from some spirit inside a bottle, something strong and sour that would obliterate any sort of sensation, any feeling at all. Her heart was sore and in need of comfort, and she wanted to forget it all, the terrifying present and the past she kept coming face to face with.

She remembered the exact date of the last time she'd drunk to forget. It was the day she'd taken the pregnancy test after realizing her period was late, very late. When the little blue line appeared, she'd disappeared into a bottle of bourbon, the only time she'd let herself go emotionally. After hours of drinking, several more of crying, and thirteen hours straight of being comatose, she'd dragged herself into the bathroom, and one look in the mirror had sobered her up. She had a baby growing inside her. Nothing else mattered, not even a broken heart.

Yet here she was, years down the road, her heart a splinter away from shattering. The beauty salon next to the bar had a wall of mirrors behind reception and Georgia caught her reflection in each one as she passed. Yesterday morning she had been getting herself ready for work and Misty ready for school, both dressing with care, both wanting to make the right impression. Her daughter had wanted to wear lipstick: Georgia told her no, she didn't need make-up, but spritzed her instead with perfume. Her own hair had been perfect, her clothes ironed and fitted. What a difference twenty-four hours could make. This morning she'd scraped her hair back into a ponytail and still wore the same clothes she'd slept in last night.

She needed to go home and shower and figure out what she needed to do next, right after she got to the drug counter and asked for the strongest medication they sold. A car squealed to a halt in front of the grocery store, the driver slamming the door as she got out.

The woman wore dark glasses but didn't remove them as she entered the store. Georgia followed her to the pharmacy. There were already people standing in a line and Georgia joined behind the woman, who was fidgety, unable to stand still, looking around.

'Karen?' Georgia gasped. Karen turned quickly, almost losing her balance. Georgia grabbed her arm to steady her. 'Are you okay?'

Karen's glassy black stare was unfathomable, making Georgia feel a little uncomfortable. She hoped Karen wasn't still moody from yesterday; she'd apologized for her insensitive question.

'Are you on a break from work?' Georgia tried again as they shuffled nearer the counter.

'I called in sick. Migraine.'

'I see.' Georgia got the sunglasses now. Her own headache was bad enough, let alone a serious migraine. It might not go down too well if she empathized with Karen, given her previous reticence to talk and the fact that she was still currently looking at the woman's back.

Karen was next to be served and she talked to the counter assistant quietly, apparently asking to speak to the pharmacist privately as she was escorted to a side room. The assistant was back to serve Georgia in a flash. 'Do you need to fill a prescription, ma'am? The pharmacist is with another customer; he'll be about fifteen minutes.'

'Just some pain relief for a headache, thank you.'

Georgia left, having purchased the tablets, but Karen was still in with the pharmacist. Surely if it was that bad, she'd see her own practitioner? Surely if it was that bad, Paul would have taken time off work to make sure he drove her? Surely if it was still a happy marriage, that was what would happen? Surely.

★　★　★

Georgia drove her car at a sedate pace along Sea Island Drive, intending to

175

head home, but not in any rush. Her rental was a little way out of town, but all that she could find at short notice. Five days in which to pack up and get across the country would phase most people; she and Misty were experts at moving. The little two-bedroom house was just fine for the two of them, really cute, with a front and back yard. Misty had been excited about that.

There really was nothing or nobody to go home for. As she left town she passed other moms in their people carriers and SUVs, headed to school to pick up their sons and daughters. The fact that she was going in the opposite direction caused her to grip the wheel tightly. Normally, bucking the system and doing things her own way gave her pleasure, but what wouldn't she give to be following every other parent of school-aged kids in River Springs to the gates, waiting for let-out when the bell rang at 2.30. Unlike all of those other parents, Georgia didn't know when her daughter would be home.

When Georgia got back to the house, she saw that there were several sheriffs' vehicles parked outside. A pair of officers nodded to her as she neared, and Officer Cross met her at the front door. 'We're just about done here, ma'am,' he said.

'Is it okay to come in?'

'Of course.'

'Did you find anything?'

'No, we didn't. Come in, Ms. Baxter. Let's have a chat.'

Georgia felt like a visitor in her own house. Half their belongings were in boxes still, all of which had been stacked neatly against the wall in the small family room. She remembered her comment to Justin earlier. They hadn't unpacked for her, but they'd left it all a lot neater than she had when she'd left for work yesterday morning. What was Justin doing now? What was he going to do with what she'd told him? She could tell that he hadn't believed her story. Did it matter that he didn't? They were nothing to each other at this point in their lives, just two people who knew each other once. What did she want him to be? Friend, father, lover? More? She'd go for friend right now, someone to help her when she didn't know where to go. But it appeared she'd have to make do with a woman called Jane Myron, to whom Cross was introducing her as she pulled her thoughts back to the present.

'Can I call you Georgia?' Jane asked her. She was all smiles and teeth.

Georgia shook her hand. 'Sure.' She smiled back, tight-lipped. This woman could only be about ten years older than Misty.

'Great. Let's take a seat and I'll tell you more about myself. I feel I already know you and Misty, just by being here.'

'Really,' Georgia mumbled.

'So as I said, I'm Jane, and I'll be your liaison officer for the duration. I can answer any questions you have or offer any advice you might need. This is my first solo outing; I just passed probation last month.' Another toothy smile, and Georgia gritted her teeth. 'We're obviously following up on interviews with the staff at the hospital. The officers are just on their way to Misty's school, now classes are over for the day. Officers are also going door to door, to both businesses and homes in the area surrounding the hospital, with Misty's photo.'

'And?'

'Tomorrow we'll need you to attend a press conference. Local stations and then affiliates will pick up the story. That way we'll have statewide coverage in a matter of hours.'

'She'll have been gone for over twenty-four hours by then. Shouldn't we do it sooner?'

'We believe the abductor to be someone in the local area, Georgia. This is a tight-knit community and we're hoping that word of mouth will produce some evidence throughout the rest of the day.'

Georgia wanted to know who 'we'

were, but instead asked, 'And what if they've taken her far away? Have you got any leads at all? Sheriff?'

'Ms. Baxter, we're following every line of inquiry that we can. We need to have a complete picture of your time here from when you arrived to the point that you saw Misty was gone.'

'I've gone over this with Justin.' Georgia caught a look between the two of them. 'Rose. He can tell you everything I told him. I have nothing to hide, Sheriff. I'll do whatever you want me to. But there's nothing else I can tell you. I just want you to find my daughter. Please.'

Officer Cross touched her arm as he stood. 'We're working on it, Ms. Baxter. I'm going to head over to the school. Jane will keep you up to speed.'

Georgia watched the older man leave and hoped that she hadn't heard doubt in his words. They didn't have a clue where Misty was. Nothing like this happened here. Justin had said so himself. How were they going to find her if they had nothing to go on? She turned to Jane, looking for reassurance from the younger woman.

'Georgia, I know you're scared.'

'Do you? How do you know how I feel?'

'I do. I've worked several missing child cases with seasoned professionals. That's why Justin requested that I join the — '

'Justin did what? When?'

'When he passed on the case he specifically asked me to work with you, because of my recent experience.'

'Which is? You just said this was your first outing.'

'After my probation, yes. But I worked on the Liam Kendrick case.'

Georgia frowned. The name rang a bell. 'The boy who went missing in Alabama,' she finally remembered.

'Yes, I worked that case.'

'He was missing for seven weeks. He was . . . ' Silence fell as Georgia contemplated the woman. The full extent of the story played itself out in her mind. 'He was dead when you found him.'

Jane's head dipped briefly. 'Indeed, Ms. Baxter. It isn't an experience I'd like to repeat.'

'And Justin recommended you?'

'Yes, ma'am.'

'Because?'

'Because he and I have worked together.'

Georgia noted the red flush starting to appear at the open neck of Jane's smart shirt. 'There haven't been any missing children cases in River Springs.'

'No, ma'am. I completed a six-month placement here earlier in the year. I worked very closely with Rose and his team on a variety of cases.'

Jane's neck turned blotchy and the color crept up into her cheeks. Georgia couldn't help but wonder whether Jane just had a crush on him or if they had actually had a relationship during her placement. She could always just ask the girl, but she remembered how it felt to be around Justin, feeling as she had about him. Female camaraderie wasn't her strong point, but she didn't want to embarrass the poor girl any more than she was already. And anyway, that wasn't Georgia's concern. She trusted Justin, and if he said Jane Myron, then Jane Myron it was.

'Okay, Jane. You tell me what I need to do and when I need to do it. I appreciate any help you can give me.' Georgia had softened her tone and was rewarded with Jane's bright smile.

An hour later Georgia waved Jane off, thankful to be alone, at least inside the house. A law enforcement officer would be on duty at all times outside of the property, available to provide assistance if she should need it. Jane had given her a pile of documents to read through, but all Georgia really wanted to do was shower and get some sleep. It seemed like days ago she had woken to find Misty gone, but the reality could still be measured in hours. The pounding in her head reminded her that she had yet to take her pain relief pills. She popped the lid off the bottle and shook two into her hand. They were the strongest that the pharmacist sold over the counter, and Georgia prayed they would do the trick. She took a swig of water from the bottle on the kitchen table and surveyed her worldly possessions in the boxes in the family room.

They wouldn't unpack themselves, and yet Georgia was reluctant to do anything with them, because it was part of the ritual of moving. She and Misty would take everything out bit by bit and decide together how their new place would look. But without her, it didn't seem right. It was just a place to sleep until Misty came home. It could wait.

★　★　★

After a long shower, Georgia dressed and came downstairs. She made herself a drink and noted the cat in the garden again. She presumed the previous occupants fed it, because it was meowing at the back door to be let in. Misty loved cats but suffered from an allergy to their fur. Georgia had let her pet it outside but not in the house, for fear of setting Misty off.

What could she give the animal to eat? Keeping a pet was never an option when Georgia had been growing up, as she'd travelled so much with her parents — not a way of living that would have been suitable for a cat or dog.

While Misty was not home, the cat would be company, and Georgia put out the rest of an opened can of tuna for it. When had the can been opened? Must have been Sunday; Misty had wanted a tuna melt for lunch. Georgia had let her daughter open the can. There had been no smooth movements; the jaws of the opener jerked and tore at the metal rather than cutting it gently. She'd warned Misty to be careful prizing the lid open.

The cat was weaving between her legs, meowing and purring alternately.

'Patience is a virtue, kitty,' Georgia muttered. The cat leaped up onto the counter, startling her. She was dimly aware of a sharp pain at the base of her thumb. A glance down showed an inch-long cut intersecting the life line on her left hand. 'Great.'

The cat continued to nudge and purr until Georgia emptied the can into a bowl. A few drops of blood fell onto the counter and she held her arm aloft to stem the flow. She could feel the blood's warmth as it trickled down her arm toward her elbow. She grabbed some paper towels and wrapped her lower arm up, mummy-like.

The cat was nearly finished, its purr threatening to rupture its voice box. It was a cute little tabby, all muscle, no fat. It must be getting fed elsewhere. There was no cat flap in the house, so if whoever lived here before them had owned it, they must have left a window open for the cat to come in and out. Georgia did so now, then turned her attention back to the boxes.

There was one that caught her attention. It had clearly been opened by the officers earlier during their search. Although it was now closed, the tape had been removed, and a bright yellow sticker denoted it as 'completed.' There were a few loose papers on top, which Georgia identified as Misty's birth certificate and her own.

If Justin's identity as Misty's father had been secret before, it was a secret no longer. Whichever officer had performed the search would have seen Justin's name on the certificate. Sure, she could have put anyone down as the father, and in the eyes of the law it meant nothing to prove that he was the father; but secrets in River Springs, once out, had a way of filtering through the populace just like a river always found its way to the sea.

Georgia wondered what Justin was doing. She'd left him with a lot to think about. She had little doubt that he would have gone directly to Paul to check out her version of events. She also had little doubt that Paul would have denied everything she said. Part of the reason that Georgia had left was to protect the man she loved, and part of it was to protect herself from the heartbreak that she was sure to have suffered if she'd stayed.

In Georgia's world, close relationships that were meant to flourish and provide support didn't exist. From an early age she'd learned that her own parents were more interested in the geological specimens they uncovered in their work than their only daughter's trials and tribulations. Promises were made but not kept; and after her parents' death when she was sixteen, every choice of friend or lover since had left her disappointed, and more often alone.

Although Justin had treated her well and told her he loved her, she had no reason to believe that he would not have sided with Paul had she stayed. He'd obviously had nearly ten years of hearing his version of events, and she had no reason to believe that now he would listen to her and take what she said as the truth. No, she could only count on herself to look after the two of them.

Opening the box to put away the paperwork, Georgia saw another box inside full of things that she had gathered, physical memories of her life to date. She didn't go into this particular box each time they moved, adding to it only when necessary. Some of the memories were painful, some happy, especially the more recent ones since Misty had been born. Georgia carefully lifted the box to the floor and sat, pulling out object after object until she was surrounded, from her parents' dig journals to Misty's first attempts at art.

Time and tears flowed as she remembered, holding each item in her hands. She opened a photo album of Misty as a baby and a toddler. She hugged the album to her chest and rocked as the tears fell. She had to get her back. She had to get her baby back.

★ ★ ★

Justin pulled up outside of Georgia's home. He'd followed the same route up Sea Island Drive, just as the sun was tucking the bright colors of her skirts away under the cover of dusk. He loved this time of day. Work was done. Normally he'd be sitting on his back porch with a cold beer, ruminating over his day and watching the sun set over the water. He loved his home, just as his parents and grandparents before him had loved it. It was too big for him alone, with no lover or kids to fill it. Things might have been so different if Georgia had stayed, but she hadn't.

He didn't like thinking about things like that. He'd done enough of it when she left, mourning what they could have had. No good would come out of what-iffing, as his momma had called it. 'What if is a no-if,' she'd say if she could hear his thoughts.

He finished a brief conversation with the sheriff's officer in the car, who reported no movement since Ms. Myron had left earlier. Jane had texted Justin just a short while ago, touching base as she hadn't seen him for a few months. Did he want to meet up for dinner? They had a lot of catching up to do, she reckoned.

Justin would have been tempted if there weren't other females vying for attention in his life, namely Georgia and Misty. Georgia had no one else she could lean on, no one else who knew her like he had once done. No one else who could understand how it felt to hold your child one day and then have her taken from you the next. He didn't want to be thinking like that. That was just another form of what-iffing; and until Georgia got Misty back safe, there could be nothing of that sort. He was not a father. She was not his child. Not yet.

The house was dark as Justin approached the front door. He rang the doorbell and waited. Georgia could be asleep. He didn't want to wake her if she was. He peered through the window to the living room. Nothing. He headed around the back of the house, noting there was no lock on the side gate. Would the cop in him ever be off duty? Would the man in him ever stop worrying about Georgia now she was back in his life?

It was dark in back too, no lights in the kitchen. The door was locked but the window was open, just a few inches. The light was fading fast, so Justin switched on the flashlight he always carried. On the floor he could see a plant had been knocked off the windowsill. There had been no breeze at all in the afternoon, no gust of wind to shift the small pot.

His heart started to pump just a little harder. The officer had said no movement, but he was only watching the front of the house. Someone could have easily gotten around the back, through a neighbor's garden. Justin silently reached through the window, his gun trained against the glass door, and found the key and twisted it awkwardly, his muscles straining as he did so. The click of the lock retracting echoed loudly in his ears. Opening the door quietly, he stepped cleanly over the spilled soil from the plant pot. He could see some items on the counter: a water bottle, and spots of . . . blood.

There was a rustle of paper followed by a scrabbling sound. Justin swung the beam of the torch further into the room, taking long steps. He trod on something that crunched underfoot. A downward flick of the flashlight revealed some white powder. He moved forward, the light picking out a couch, boxes, papers strewn around, legs . . .

'Georgia?' he whispered. 'What the . . .' A wail took his attention as something jumped up onto the kitchen counter, knocking over the water bottle. A cat hissed at him and then ran past him to the open back door. Justin dropped to his knees next to Georgia, who was lying on the floor on her front, her head buried in her arms.

'Georgia.' He grasped her shoulders and shook her gently. There was no resistance in her body. 'Georgia? Georgia, can you hear me?'

8

'You scared the cat,' she mumbled, lifting her head, her hair all over her face.

'What are you doing on the floor? Are you hurt?' Justin shone the light in her face and then clicked it off as she squinted.

'I'm fine. I was just going through some things.'

He helped her to her feet, supporting her as she didn't seem to be able to stand. Once she was sitting on the couch, he crossed to the wall to find the light switch.

'Where's the cat?' She shaded her eyes with her hand.

'It ran. Forget the cat.'

'I cried all over it but it just kept purring. Misty loves cats.'

Was she slurring, or was it just him? He took her face in his hands, looking at her eyes. Her pupils were pinpricks. 'Have you been drinking? Have you taken something?'

'Yes.'

Her breath didn't smell of anything other than mint, so unless she'd been quaffing crème de menthe, she'd brushed her teeth fairly recently. 'What have you taken?'

'Ibuprofen.' She pointed at a tablet bottle that was open on the counter next to the water bottle, its contents spilled.

'How many have you taken?'

Georgia frowned at him. Was she understanding him? *Please, God, say she hasn't tried to overdose.* 'Georgia, how many?' He raised his voice and shook her again. She swatted at him ineffectively and he noticed blood-soaked paper towels on her wrist.

'Two. Stop shouting. You'll make my headache worse.'

'Are you sure?'

'Justin, I'm an adult. I can read the dosage on a bottle of headache tablets.'

'What's this on your wrist? You've haven't tried to . . . ' He couldn't bring himself to say the words.

'I cut myself on a can of tuna. Stop fussing.'

'Sorry. I was just . . . '

She was still frowning at him as he carefully stepped backwards, avoiding all the things on the floor. It looked like an indoor garage sale.

'Do you want a hand putting these things away?' If she wasn't going to let him be concerned about her, surely something more practical wouldn't get her back up any more.

Her attention was on piles of books, papers, and all manner of objects. She was getting that glazed-over look again. He squatted so he was in her line of vision, and picked up a leather-bound book. 'Did the sheriff's office leave all of this out?'

'No, they put everything back neat and tidy. I just wanted to go through some stuff to try and feel closer to Misty. She's only been gone a few hours, and I'm starting to forget what she looks like.'

'Of course you're not. You're just tired and out of kilter.'

'But the longer she's gone . . . ' Georgia left the words unsaid, pulling her knees up to her chest. 'What are you doing here?'

'I wanted to see how you were. Let me look at that cut.'

'I'm fine, honestly. I just need to get the room straightened out and get some sleep.'

Justin saw no need to comment on that. He left her hugging her knees while he moved around the room, picking everything up off the floor and piling it up on the boxes. A photo album was open, showing pictures of what could only be Misty when she was a baby. He swallowed back an unknown feeling and quickly shut the book. Now was not the time to fill in the gaps in his daughter's childhood.

Too late, obviously, he was already referring to her as his daughter. To refute that he believed Georgia's claim would be like shutting the stable door after the horse had bolted and won the Kentucky Derby. If he was honest, he'd done nothing but think of the little girl he'd held briefly yesterday. She been in his thoughts all day — at work, at the gym at lunchtime, and most certainly now, in the same room as Georgia and surrounded by her things.

Could he do this? Could he be the friend that Georgia so clearly needed? Could he suspend everything that had happened between them over the years and just concentrate on finding Misty? He glanced over his shoulder at Georgia, who was biting her thumbnail, tears brimming in her eyes. She needed someone, and if it was to be him, then so be it. He might not be involved in the case in any official capacity, but he was involved emotionally — with Georgia, and the child who might or might not be his. He *was* involved.

'Would you like to come over for a

few hours? Have some dinner?' he asked.

Georgia looked up at him, a tear rolling down her cheek. 'Thank you, but I'm fine.'

'The hell you are, Georgia.' He pulled her up and told her to go splash water on her face while he locked up. 'We'll eat, talk, whatever, but you're not spending the night alone.'

She followed his instructions without demur and he set about locking the back door and window. His phone beeped again — another message from Jane asking about dinner. He sent back 'Sorry, I have plans,' and left it at that. Georgia was higher on his list of priorities just now. Jane would have to wait.

* * *

Justin scooted up to make space for Georgia as she joined him on the sofa, out on the back porch. She'd made him go sit outside while she finished stacking the dishwasher and made coffee. They'd made dinner together, despite his insistence that she just sit and relax. He guessed if she kept busy, she didn't have time to think about Misty. The girl was in his thoughts already and he'd only met her once. How was it for Georgia?

If he wanted to torture himself a little more, he could pretend like it was just yesterday she lived here with him. The way she had moved around the kitchen and around him as they prepared dinner, it could be ten years ago. She automatically knew where the cutlery and crockery were. Perhaps it was easy for her to slip back into their routine, or perhaps it was that he was a creature of habit and everything was in the same place as it was then.

They sat side by side in silence, almost touching but not. This would be so easy if he just let it happen, as if nothing had changed. He was aware of the delicate sips she took of her coffee. She always was impatient, never wanting to wait.

How difficult was it, then, for her to have to wait for news of Misty?

'So, how was your day?' Georgia asked. A simple question, but Justin found it hard not to remember how many nights they'd sat out when it warm enough and had this same conversation. She'd be waiting for him when he'd finished a shift, wanting to know what he'd been up to at work.

'Oh, you know, the usual.' He quirked a smile. 'Ex-lover comes back to town, yada yada yada.'

'You must mean Ms. Myron.' She was teasing him, but he didn't feel inclined to discuss Jane.

'Aforementioned ex-lover gets stuck in the elevator. Her child is in a car wreck.'

'That was yesterday.'

'Aforementioned child gets abducted and I'm told I'm a father.' He met her eyes over the top of her cup as she took a sip. He didn't know why he'd said all that. But that was how his day had gone, pretty much.

'Big day, huh?'

'As it goes, yeah. How was yours?'

Georgia nodded. 'Pretty much the same as yours.'

'How you holding up?' Justin reached out and cupped the back of her neck. She'd put her hair up when they'd made dinner. She tensed and then relaxed slightly, but her muscles were tight. He saw her eyes close just for a brief second as his hand made contact, and the tiniest sigh escaped her lips.

'I'm lost.' Just two words and he understood everything she was saying.

'I'm here.' He gently rubbed her neck with his fingertips, using gentle pressure, easing the knots he felt. She was as beautiful now as she was then, and as much as he knew he shouldn't, he wanted to hold her, to love her. Even for all that she'd hurt him, pride be damned, he wanted her still.

He took the cup from her, placed it on the floor, and took her hand. She gazed at him for a long moment and he waited. He couldn't take the kiss from her this time; she had to be willing to give. Why did he want this woman so much? She'd hurt him, and now she was back with more trouble than he could have imagined.

He released her hand and began to move his own hand from her neck, but she grabbed both of his tightly.

'I loved you, Justin.'

'But?'

'I can't start anything, no matter what it might be. Not while Misty is missing. Please know it's not because I don't want to, but now's not the time to be thinking about you and me.'

Justin cupped her cheek and smoothed her hair back from her face. 'It's too late, hun. I already have.' He stood up and walked to the veranda steps. And she'd shut him down. What did he expect? He didn't know whether to be angry at her for making him feel like a complete idiot, or at himself for expecting her to focus on anything other than Misty. He just wanted to make it right for her, even for a few minutes.

'What did you just say?' Her voice was a cold whisper.

'It doesn't matter now.'

'No, what did you say?'

'It's okay. You made yourself clear.'

'Justin, tell me what you said.' Her raised voice made him turn. She was out of the seat and before him in a single step. 'Tell me. Please?'

'I said it's too late. I've already — '

'It's too late. It's too late.' Her hands flew to her head and she began pacing up and down. 'Someone else said that to me. Who was it? Ugh, remember, remember.' She paced and muttered, her hands clasped tightly to her head. Then she stopped and stared at the roof, mumbling those same words over and over.

'Georgia, you're scaring me. What's wrong?'

'Someone said that to me last night. At the hospital.'

'Who? When last night?'

'I don't know.' She turned panicked eyes to him. 'I can't remember. Does it mean anything?'

'Think. Was it before or after you caught up with Tracy?' He caught her hands and drew her to sit down on the steps. 'Think about what you were doing when they said it.'

'It was after Tracy went, and Misty was sleeping. I hadn't finished the drink Tracy bought for me.'

'What was the drink?'

'It was coffee.'

'And then what happened next?'

'I drank it, because I was really thirsty. It was only just about warm. I checked on Misty and then sat down in the chair.'

'What was happening around you? Do you know what time it was? I think you said Tracy left at . . . ' Justin let his voice trail off. He recognized the look on her face. She was concentrating hard, trying to recall.

'It was a little after nine, about quarter after. I looked at my phone. I was tired, really tired.'

'You were sitting in the chair just to

the left of Misty's bed.' He'd memorized the layout of the hospital room when he was there earlier that morning.

'I must have dozed off.'

'In the chair? And yet you woke up on the cot they provided for you. How did you get there if you were asleep in the chair?' He was careful not to put any assumptions forward, not wanting to throw her off track. She was doing just fine, but asking the questions would allow her subconscious to fill in the gaps.

A variety of expressions worked their way across Georgia's face as she played it back in her mind. 'Someone called my name, but it was dark.'

'What was their voice like?'

'It was a whisper.'

'Were they close to you or far away?'

She closed her eyes and a frown creased her brow. Justin knew she didn't know the answer, but was trying to work it through.

'I didn't open my eyes. I couldn't.'

'Why couldn't you?'

'I tried. My eyelids were heavy. I couldn't move. Everything was just so heavy.'

'Good, hun, good. What next? Did they talk to you some more?'

'She was shaking me. She said I should go to bed.'

'But everything was heavy. You couldn't move.'

'She helped me.'

'You're doing great. Can you remember anything else?' Justin squeezed her hands to encourage her.

'I asked what the time was.'

'And she said . . . ?'

'It's quarter after ten.'

Justin remained silent, waiting for her to come back to him. It took a few seconds until she refocused, her eyes wide. He smoothed her knuckles with his thumbs. 'I want you to finish your coffee. I need to call Cross with this.' He paused before he stood. 'Are you okay?'

She nodded, her teeth worrying at her top lip. He passed her drink and dropped a kiss on her head before heading into the kitchen to use the phone, pausing at the door as she spoke.

'Is it important? Will it help?' Her voice caught on a shuddered breath.

'I think it might.'

* * *

'Sheriff, it's Rose. I'm sorry to disturb you at home.'

'Rose. I hear you've been spending time with Ms. Baxter. Do you have something for me?'

'Yes, sir. She remembers something from last night. Tracy Goodwin left at approximately nine-fifteen p.m. and Georgia felt tired and fell asleep in the chair. Someone came into Misty's room at approximately ten-fifteen p.m. and helped Georgia get into bed.'

'Does Ms. Baxter know who it was?'

'No. She recalls being very lethargic; her eyes were heavy and she couldn't get them to open. I believe she may have been drugged. Tracy got them both a coffee and she made a point of telling Georgia that she should be sure to drink it.'

'We'll need to review the CCTV from last night. I'll arrange for the night shift to be questioned again. The trash from the last twenty-four hours has been kept on site; I'll get a team to start sifting through looking for disposable cups. Good work, Justin. We've had jack-shit to go on so far. We need a break and this might just be it.'

'Thanks, Sheriff. I think it might be worth doing a tox screen on Georgia to see if there's anything in her system still.'

'Sure. I'll send a technician now, and someone will be over to take a statement.'

'We're at my house, sir.'

'Son, I wouldn't be doing my job if I didn't know that, now, would I?'

'No, sir.'

Officer Cross chuckled and Justin grinned sheepishly. 'I'll get on it right away, Detective Rose, and then you and Ms. Baxter can get on with your evening. I'll be in touch first thing.'

★   ★   ★

Georgia stood when she heard Justin come out to the veranda and smiled when she saw he was carrying another cup of coffee. 'Thank you. Did you get through to Cross?' She took the drink gratefully, the warmth from the cup seeping into her fingers. The evening was growing chilly.

'I did. He's going to send an officer over to take a statement, just for the record. He's also getting officers back to interview the night shift again tonight, and he'll obviously have last night's CCTV monitored.'

'Do you think they'll find anything?'

'I don't know, but it's worth a try. They'd like to do a blood test. You might have been drugged so whoever it was could take Misty.'

'Drugged?' Georgia blew out a

breath. 'Someone planned this, didn't they?'

'It would take some planning,' he said, nodding. 'As we didn't get any clues from the CCTV during that specific timeframe, we should get something from earlier. That corridor is covered from end to end.'

'Why didn't they check last night's tapes?'

'Because of the five a.m. round. These bed checks are there for a reason and are signed off by the attending doctor. What you remember from last night changes things; gives us more scope.'

'And Tracy?' Justin shrugged. 'Do you think she has Misty? Will the police go over there now?'

'There's no evidence that she's involved. We can't just go around accusing people.'

'But . . .'

'It's natural to want to go charging in, even on the smallest hint of a lead, but there are procedures to follow.

Trust in them. Every lead is followed up, and the investigators will keep us posted.'

He'd said 'us.' Georgia took every little piece of hope she could, storing a word, a look, a touch away for the future, in case she needed to build a wall. Whether that was to keep Justin in or out was yet to be seen.

'I do trust you,' she said, but he didn't act like he'd noticed her words. 'I just want Misty back.'

'Of course; that's what we all want.'

'I want her to get to know you.'

Justin faltered for just a second, a flash of something crossing his face, and Georgia felt him move backwards ever so slightly, backing off. A tight smile told her he was shutting down on her. She needed him, and she wasn't going to lose him before she had him.

'Will the officer be here soon? I'd like to go home and get some sleep. Everything's catching up with me.' She deliberately turned and moved away, to let him know she wasn't going to press him, and entered the house. He had some thinking and adjusting to do. In Justin's world, actions spoke louder than words, and his trust would be something she would have to gain. Anything other than friend right now would have to wait, for both of them. She had fast begun to depend on him to help her navigate this nightmare, and knew she couldn't do it alone.

Georgia loaded the dishwasher and turned it on. Funny how she felt comfortable, here of all places. She'd lived most other places in her life longer than she'd lived here with Justin, but it was the only place she'd ever thought of as home. He hadn't changed anything much, and most of the furniture had been in the family for generations. It had been his grandparents' house, then his parents', and he was proud of his family history. It was such a shame that his parents hadn't lived to see their boy succeed.

Justin's voice filtered through the kitchen door. Georgia wondered if he was talking on the phone. His voice was low and she couldn't make out the words. Perhaps the officer had arrived to take her statement. Best get it over with, then she could go home. Justin had driven her, so she'd be reliant on someone taking her back. She had to stop using local law enforcement as a taxi service. A second voice joined his and Georgia took that as her cue, calling out as she went outside, so she didn't disturb their conversation.

'Officer, do you want to come inside? We can sit at the table, if you don't mind.' She stopped, her fingers on the edge of the screen door. 'Or I can come back later.'

Justin and the officer hadn't heard her. The officer was Jane Myron, and she was pressed against Justin, her lips on his.

Georgia's stomach muscles clenched. She set the screen door silently back into the frame, stepping to the side so that she didn't have to look at the two of them. She knew she had no right to

215

interfere with whatever Justin had going on with the young woman; he'd said he'd moved on, and she could see that with her own eyes. Jane was kissing Justin with vigor, her hands splayed against his chest. Georgia remembered how that felt, pressed against his hard body, wanting him so much, loving him so deeply that she wished she could stay like that forever. But she had no right to remember, no claim on Justin apart from the fact that he was Misty's father; and even there, she was on rocky ground.

The doorbell rang, pulling Georgia from her memories. Her heart raced with anticipation of some news of her daughter, but then she recalled that an officer was on the way to take a statement. Leaving Justin to his other visitor, she opened the front door, determined to stay focused on what really mattered: doing all she could to find Misty.

★ ★ ★

Justin was antsy and he didn't know why. He couldn't stay still, pacing the room, sitting then standing, the whole time that Officer Michaels was talking quietly to Georgia in the lounge room. Their hushed tones bothered him; he wanted to know exactly what Michaels was asking her. But he didn't interrupt, as Georgia looked like she was concentrating hard on remembering, just like she had when he'd encouraged her to go over the events of the night before.

Georgia was focused on what she was saying to the officer; she appeared not to notice that Justin was gazing at her, willing her to look at him. In fact, she seemed to be studiously ignoring both him and Jane. Justin was also trying to ignore Jane, but she seemed determined to stay.

When the doorbell had rung earlier, Justin had tried to extricate himself from Jane's grasping hands. Her kisses, which he'd welcomed just a few months ago, did nothing for him this evening, and the more he'd tried to push her away, the more desperately she'd held onto him. It was only the sound of Michaels and Georgia talking that had broken her hold, allowing Justin to put some distance between them. Since then, she'd trotted after him, sad brown eyes following his every move. That was why he'd kept moving, worried that if he settled in one place long enough, Jane might physically attach herself to him again. He knew he was over-dramatizing the situation, but could the two women in his house be more polarized? One was desperate to be near him, the other apparently not.

Georgia's silent demur to his offer of a ride home after the officer had concluded his questions told him the shutters were down, at least for tonight. She met his gaze briefly over the top of the officer's car and he wanted to read something else in those few seconds, other than the overwhelming sadness that he saw. He shouldn't be letting her go home to an empty house. She didn't know where her daughter was, and she was going to be alone. He stood on the front porch watching the squad car disappear into the night, hands in the pockets of his jeans. Suddenly he sensed Jane behind him, and as she snaked her arms around his torso his fists balled, tightly clenched, matching the tension in his jaw.

'Alone at last,' she murmured, her cheek against his back. He could feel the warmth of her breath and the movement of her lips through his T-shirt. 'Let's go inside, Justin. I need you to hold me.'

Justin tried to stop the shiver that her words conjured. He knew exactly what she meant; what she expected was going to happen. But he couldn't lie down with Jane — not tonight; not ever again. The shiver started small but built to a tremor very quickly. Jane felt the ripple of his muscles and he heard the smile in her voice.

'Are you cold? Let me warm you up.'

The shudder became stronger. There was no way he could do this, not with her. His mind was elsewhere, his thoughts on the woman who still held his heart and the little girl who was out there somewhere — both alone, both scared — and he wanted to make it better for them. He'd foregone the chance to investigate Misty's disappearance, but he'd be damned if he'd give up the chance to be with Georgia, especially after tonight. There was still a gaping hole in his life, so many years after she'd left him. But she was back, and there was a hole in her life — in her heart too, without Misty — and she needed someone. She needed him.

With a sharp intake of breath, Justin turned to Jane. He knew she wanted him, but it was no good. She wasn't Georgia.

9

Justin rubbed his jaw as he drove. Jane had damn near broken it when he'd told her that nothing was going to happen between them, and that he didn't want to see her again. For someone so petite, she sure knew how to slug a guy. The conversation had taken less than two minutes from start to finish, and most of that was Jane screaming at him, following him through the house as he locked up. He knew he hadn't handled it very well, but he wanted to get to Georgia as fast as he could.

He pulled up outside her house, just as the officer pulled off. Michaels nodded to him before driving away. Justin knew his presence would raise some eyebrows in the sheriff's office tomorrow, but it was too late to change that now. It had been a hell of a day so far, and he didn't anticipate it being any less eventful as he knocked on the door.

★ ★ ★

Georgia's pounding heart seemingly anticipated Justin's pounding fist. As she leaned against the front door, she was sure his knocking was making her body shake. She'd seen him pull up as she closed the door to the officer, waiting until he was in his car to shut the door.

Justin knocked again, and Georgia turned her head, resting her cheek against the wood. What did he want with her now? It was gone eleven and she was exhausted, but she wasn't sure she would sleep even if she did go to bed. Every strand of her being was calling out for her daughter. How could she even close her eyes when she had no idea where her baby was, who she was with, if she was safe? A sob escaped her lips and her hand flew to cover her mouth. If she was quiet, he might go away.

'Georgia, I can hear you. Let me in, please?'

She shook her head, her hand tight to her face, but sob followed sob.

'Hun, open the door. You don't have to do this alone.'

Georgia moved her hand to the door latch, closing her eyes. The image of Misty that she had been trying to keep at the forefront of her mind all day came as clearly as if she was standing in front of her. But in place of the smiling, happy girl Georgia knew her to be appeared a crouched, disheveled little girl, scared and dirty, tears smudging a path down her cheek. The little girl's lips were moving, but there was no sound to accompany the nightmare picture unfolding in her mind — *Mommy, Mommy?*

A low keening began deep inside her and she listened as the noise built, reverberating in her chest, squeezing the air from her lungs, stinging her throat as the sound rose to her mouth.

The moan drew on her last reserves of strength; her arms and shoulders suddenly became leaden and her legs shook, incapable of holding her upright any longer. Her grip on the door latch tightened; she managed to open the door before she buckled, folding like a marionette puppet, frayed strings snapping, disjointed limbs collapsing in slow motion.

The door slammed shut under her weight, the thud registering somewhere in her subconscious. Alone was what she should be. Justin had given up, left her to herself, just like she'd left him in the dark of the night. Was it dark where Misty was?

'I've got you.'

A whisper from the darkness. Georgia repeated the words, her voice hoarse, her eyes closed. She imagined she was looking down on Misty, curled on the floor; she scooped her up. How had she forgotten how easy it was to lift her and carry her? How long had it been since she'd held her baby in her arms? How long since she'd felt her child's breath against her neck as she carried her up to bed?

Georgia could feel the pressure of a body against hers and the sway of that body as it moved, as they moved. She squeezed her eyes tight, not wanting to admit what she already knew. She wasn't the one doing the carrying, taking her precious daughter up to bed after she'd fallen asleep on the couch. She was the one being carried. She wasn't the one who was pressing her lips to her child's golden hair, murmuring words of love and goodnight. She was the one being kissed; she was the one being comforted. She wasn't the one who felt her daughter's arms around her neck, holding her tight. She was the one being held.

The swaying had stopped lulling her into believing what wasn't true. Justin had scooped her up from the floor and carried her up the stairs. He paused at the top, turning slightly to the left, then to the right, his muscles flexing, obviously trying to ascertain which room was hers.

'You can put me down, Justin. I'm okay.' She raised her gaze. He looked like he didn't believe her; that frown was back again. Would he ever smile at her? 'Put me down, please.'

'Are you sure? You don't look okay.'

She blew her hair off her face and swiped her hand across her eyes. 'Thanks. Listen, as much as I appreciate your support, you don't need to be here. I'm just going to take a shower and go to bed. I guess I've got to do a press conference tomorrow, and maybe the sheriff's department will need me to answer more questions after I give my statement.'

Still he hadn't put her down. 'I know you don't mean that. I bet this is the first night you've ever been away from Misty, isn't it?'

Georgia's breath caught in her throat and she ducked her head from his gaze. She didn't want him to see her cry. How did he know that? Not one single night had Misty been apart from her;

and yet here Justin was, nine years' worth of nights apart between them, and he could still read her. How was that? She asked the question aloud without realizing.

Justin lowered her until her feet touched the floor, but he didn't release her completely. 'I can't answer that, Georgia. I don't know you anymore, and I don't know Misty at all, but there's just something . . . '

He didn't need to finish because Georgia knew exactly what he meant. Was it that their love had been so deep, there was still something between them? Yes was her answer, but she couldn't vouch for him. She still loved him; theirs was an unfinished story, one that was still being written.

She knew there was something the moment she'd heard his voice yesterday when he'd prized the elevator door open. She'd felt that something when he'd put his hand through and told her to take it, his skin as warm as it ever was. It was there in every touch, every look; in his kiss, his voice, everything. That was what he was to her still — everything. But there was nothing but secrets, lies, and a missing child to hold them together.

'You should go home,' Georgia said feebly. She didn't really want him to go. She just wanted him to hold her, to make it all right. She wanted him to find their daughter so he could know just how amazing his little girl was.

'I don't want to.' His hand was on her hair now, smoothing it back from her face, making her look at him.

'You need to.'

'I need to do a lot of things, and going home isn't one of them, Georgia.'

'But Jane . . . '

Justin squeezed her tight with his arm around her waist and held her head, his palm curling around her neck below her ear. 'Jane what? She's not here. It's just you and me.'

'But . . . '

'No buts, hun. Don't let there be anything between us tonight — not what's happened, or what's going to happen. It's been a hell of a day for you.' He pressed a thumb to her lips when she began to protest. 'And it's been a hell of a day for me too. Whatever is right or wrong, can we just forget it? Just for tonight?'

'Misty . . . I should be . . . '

'What are you going to do at this time of night? Everything that can be done is being done. There'll be much more of the same as soon as it's light, but there's nothing to do now. Believe me, if there was, I'd be doing it.'

Georgia wanted to push him away. Misty was alone, God knew where, and Georgia wanted to suffer the same.

'She's my daughter, too, isn't she?' he continued. Georgia nodded. 'Then she needs for both of us to be strong, for whatever comes. Neither of us will be fit for anything if we stay up all night and tear our hair out, frustrated that we know nothing more than we did this morning. But you did really well this evening, Georgia. You remembered things, and those things could lead in all sorts of directions.'

'You think?'

'I know.' He pressed his lips to hers briefly. 'I may not be able to investigate this officially, but I can be here for you, and I can be here for Misty when she comes home.' He kissed her again and Georgia opened her mouth to say something, but his lips took any words she was going to speak.

* * *

A phone was ringing, distantly at first, but soon it became louder, more insistent, like it was demanding to be answered. Justin registered it was his phone, but didn't feel inclined to answer it. He'd been enjoying a deep sleep and reluctantly rolled onto his back.

'Justin, aren't you going to answer it?' Georgia's voice came from the darkness next to him, gentle yet sleepy, and his eyes opened.

'Go back to sleep, hun. I've got it.' He sat up, reaching for his phone on the night stand with one hand and touching Georgia with the other, her skin warm and soft. He hadn't been dreaming.

He pressed 'answer' without seeing what number was displayed on the screen. 'Justin Rose.'

'Bro, I've been knocking loud enough to wake the dead. *Are* you dead?' Paul's voice slurred down the phone line, followed by a loud cackle.

'No, I'm not. Paul, do you know what time it is?'

'Hell, jus' let me in. *Mi casa, su casa.* That's what you said today.'

'Where are you?' Justin tried to keep his voice down, but his friend irritated the hell out of him when he did this. 'Did Karen kick you out again?'

'She won't let me in the house. Let me in. Back door's locked. I'm at the front door.'

'You're at mine?'

'Where else? *Mi casa, su casa.*'

'I'm not there, P.'

'Where you at? Work? What's the emergency this time? Cat stuck in a tree?' Raucous laughter came again.

'Who is it, Justin? Is it about Misty?' Georgia mumbled next to him.

'Shh, darlin', go back to sleep.'

'You keeping company, bro?' Paul whistled. 'Who is it? Jane?'

'No. Just go to the motel.'

'Nah, come home, bro. Let's get loaded.'

'No, Paul. Go get some sleep. You can't keep doing this.' Justin felt Georgia wriggling beside him as he hissed into the phone.

'Come on, man. I need you. Who's more important, me or some broad?'

'I'm not getting into this now. I'll see you tomorrow.'

'It's that bitch, ain't it? Sexy freakin' Sweets? Christ, man, didn't you get hurt enough first time around?' Paul's voice came loud and clear down the line.

'Goodnight, Paul.'

232

'Justin, she's trouble. Keep the hell away from her.'

'I said — '

'I'll get you, you bitch!' Justin had to hold the phone away from his ear as Paul began to scream. 'Just you wait, you'll get yours! I'll — '

Justin pressed 'end' on the call and put the phone back on the table, waiting for Georgia to say something, but all he could hear was her breathing. What could he say? With his professional head on, all his training told him to look at the evidence. Who of the two had left without a word and who had stayed, been there through thick and thin? But Paul's destructive behavior had been steadily getting worse for years, and no amount of pleading or arguing had any effect.

'He's out of control, Georgia.' He turned to her in the darkness and pulled her into his arms, feeling her breath against his shoulder as he hugged her and the dampness on her cheek.

'He's always been out of control,' she whispered, and then shook her head when Justin asked what she meant. 'I can't think about him anymore, Justin. It's a waste of time and energy that I need to save to get through this, until we find Misty.'

Justin closed his eyes and slid down against the pillows, bringing Georgia with him. 'We will.' He kissed her softly and pulled her closer. He couldn't think about Paul either, but the phone call had left a bad taste in his mouth, and he wasn't sure that any amount of Georgia's sweetness was going to get rid of it anytime soon.

★ ★ ★

'Coming,' Georgia called as she headed to the door. Someone was knocking insistently.

'Hi, Georgia.' Jane stood on the doorstep with a breezy smile. 'I hope I didn't wake you?'

'No, no, come in. I've been up for a

little while now.' Georgia stood back to let her in. She wondered if she'd passed Justin on the way up the highway from River Springs, but nothing in the young woman's demeanor gave any indication that she knew he'd spent the night.

'How are you feeling today? I hope you got a good night's sleep?' She gave Georgia a sidelong glance and then qualified her question. 'As good as you can in these circumstances. I'm sure you're going through a whole gamut of emotions. It's only natural.'

'I did okay, thanks. So what do you need me to do today? Would you like a drink? Coffee? Come on through.' She led the way to the kitchen and gestured for Jane to take a seat at the counter.

'Sure, coffee would be great, thanks.'

'You're welcome.' Georgia poured a cup, passed it to Jane, and then waited. Jane added milk to the cup, but just continued to smile. 'So, today?' Georgia prompted her.

'I'm afraid it's going to be a busy day. First of all, we need you to take a polygraph test. It's being set up at the sheriff's office, so as soon as you're ready we'll head there. The CCTV footage has been reviewed, and there are a few anomalies that need to be cleared up, but Officer Cross will meet with you to talk you through it all. There are a few leads that we're ready to follow from the information that you provided to Officer Michaels last night, and the toxicology report is due back on your blood sample in the next couple of hours.'

Georgia couldn't stop herself from grinning as Jane talked. 'That's fantastic. We might find Misty soon.'

Jane gave her a smile and patted her hand. Georgia felt suitably patronized. 'It is progress,' Jane said, 'but we've yet to prove these are warm leads. These things can take time.'

'But Misty doesn't have time. She's been gone so long already. I read the information you gave me yesterday, and the first forty-eight hours are crucial.'

'Which is why we've also called a

press conference for ten o'clock. It'll be televised live through local TV and radio stations, and will be picked up by the syndicates. The press have been invited as well, and they'll update their websites and blogs as soon as it's over. Today's media moves quickly, so we expect to have this statewide by lunchtime.'

Georgia wrapped her hands around her mug, a shiver running through her body. The idea of everyone knowing that her daughter was missing was unnerving. It would put her in the spotlight, when for most of her life she'd managed to stay under the radar, just plain old Georgia. It seemed it was only in River Springs that she was destined to be known, and not always for a good reason. People would stare at her, feel sorry for her, pity her and judge her: 'There's the woman whose daughter was in a road traffic accident and ended up in hospital.' 'There's the woman whose daughter was abducted while she slept.'

'Are you okay, Georgia? I'm sorry that you have to do these things today, but it's essential. Do you need to bring anyone with you, to support you?'

Georgia was a little bothered to see the other woman narrow her eyes at the last question, and wondered if she was challenging her to name Justin. The thought had crossed her mind, but she had to do this alone. While she knew that Justin was Misty's father, he only had her word for it. After all, this was his home town, and Georgia owed him the chance to be a father on whatever terms he chose, rather than forcing his hand before he'd even had time to fall in love with their little girl.

'No,' Georgia replied. 'You'll be there at the press conference, won't you?'

Jane's eyes widened at Georgia's question and she smiled brightly, with a nod.

'Then I'm good.' Georgia swallowed the last of her coffee and stood. 'Let's do this.'

The polygraph test proved to be the same questions Georgia had already been asked, just by a different person in a different room. She was wired up to a machine that would put Misty's etch-a-sketch to shame and was nervous all the way through the test, but the gentleman who asked the questions announced to Officer Cross and all assembled that she was telling the truth.

The CCTV footage was a different matter. Justin had joined them by this time; and as Cross explained that his team had watched the tapes from seven o'clock on the Monday night through to seven the following morning, he reached for her hand and held it tight.

'What I want you to watch is a half-hour period from four-thirty a.m. through to five a.m.,' Cross told her. 'We'll watch it in two sections, then we'll discuss what it means as far as the investigation's concerned. The tape is set to double speed for the first ten minutes. Okay?'

Georgia nodded and duly looked at the grainy color picture on the large monitor mounted on the wall. They were in the control room, surrounded by lots of flashing lights and beeping sounds, along with other monitors showing footage of traffic and security cameras around town. She tried to concentrate, but the high-speed footage was making her feel nauseous. There was little to look at on the screen, which showed a shot of a long corridor with doors on either side. In the middle of the corridor on the left-hand side, from this particular camera angle, was the nurses' station. After a few minutes Officer Cross signaled for the tape to be paused.

'Ms. Baxter, please note the time is now four thirty-eight a.m. according to the CCTV — see in the corner?'

'Yes.'

'And note that you and your daughter were asleep in this room, here.' Cross used a laser pointer to indicate the door to their room. 'This room is the nearest to the nurses' station from this particular angle.'

'Okay.' Georgia frowned as the tape restarted. She watched as the nurse left the room next to Misty's and then entered Misty's room. Georgia's gaze flicked to the time stamp in the bottom right-hand corner of the screen. It read 4:41 a.m. Justin noticed the same and they exchanged a look.

The tape now ran at normal speed and the nurse left Misty's room at 4:43 a.m. Georgia opened her mouth to say something but Justin squeezed her hand and shook his head. On the screen, the door at the far end of the corridor opened and the nurse, by now back at the nurses' station, greeted the doctor with a hug. They stood and talked for a minute and then the doctor followed the nurse behind the desk, where she reached under it for something. The lights all along the corridor went out.

Georgia tried to make sense of what

she was seeing. The corridor was illuminated by emergency lights, making it very difficult to make out doorways and even the nurses' station. A light flared briefly as the nurse opened the door to a lit office behind the desk, then both she and the doctor entered the room and shut the door, and the corridor was cloaked in gloom again. The time stamp on screen read 4:46 a.m.

Officer Cross raised his hand to pause the tape. 'Okay, Ms. Baxter?'

'Call me Georgia, please. I'm not sure I understand what happened. Do the lights get turned out between bed checks, to save energy?'

'No. The lights in the corridors should stay on throughout the night; only lights in the patients' rooms are turned down low or turned off.'

'Then why did she turn the lights out?'

'Good question. We asked the nurse the same question when we caught her coming off duty at nine this morning. In fact, we asked her several questions.

You'll note the time that she exited your daughter's room after doing the five a.m. bed check?'

'The time's wrong on the CCTV,' Justin interjected before Georgia could speak. 'Or the time's right, and the bed check was done early.'

Georgia raised her eyebrows in surprise. 'Why would they write it up as five a.m. then?'

'Rose is right,' Cross said. 'The nurse in question tearfully admitted that every third week, when working the night shift, she does the five a.m. bed check early. She's been having an affair with the on-call doctor that you saw on screen for about six months. Unfortunately, the doctor is still operating as we speak; but rest assured, we have an officer waiting to interview him the moment he leaves the OR.'

'So what does that mean? How long were they in the office?'

'Only twelve minutes, and you can see a close-up of their faces in a little while to see if you recognize them, just to rule them out of our investigation. The nurse's story is consistent with what we can see on CCTV, but we'll have to see if the doctor will corroborate it.'

'Sure, but it was all a bit of a blur on Monday. The only people I can place are Tracy Davidson, a nurse called Cassie, and Doctor Hurricane.'

'Hurricane?' Cross and Justin said at the same time.

'Oh, what was his name? Harrison. He talked up a storm and then disappeared.'

'Well, let me show you the rest of the tape, then we can do the ID,' Cross said.

The tape started again and Georgia strained her eyes to watch the gloom. Nothing changed, just the odd flicker of the emergency lighting, until a door opened on the other side of the corridor from the nurses' station. It remained ajar for a short while before a figure emerged.

'Who's that?' Georgia leaned forward to see.

'Keep watching,' Cross spoke quietly.

In the darkened corridor, a long-haired person wearing pants and a short-sleeved top closed the door. Their back was to the camera as they sidestepped across to the other wall. They looked quickly behind the nurses' station and then disappeared into Misty's room.

'Is that them? Is that who took my baby?' Georgia stood and walked closer to the screen, but all she was looking at were pixels in differing shades of gray.

'Sit down, Georgia,' Cross told her. 'There's more to see.'

On screen, the person went back across the corridor, opened the door they had come through, and pulled out something on wheels. It looked to be a folded-up wheelchair. They went back into Misty's room and exited at 4:55 a.m., pushing a wheelchair, which now had someone in it.

'Misty!' Georgia whispered and got up once more to press her nose to the screen, watching the blurred image of her daughter disappearing down the corridor, through the double doors and out of sight. Tears ran freely down her cheeks as she stood stock still, until movement on the screen a minute later followed by a flare of bright light hurt her eyes, and she took a step back. The doctor and nurse had exited the office, and the lights in the corridor were turned back on. After a furtive check up and down the corridor, the doctor gave the nurse a long kiss and then followed the same path as the abductor and disappeared from view.

Cross had an officer pause the tape; the time stamp showed 5:03 a.m., three minutes after the supposed time the nurse had performed the bed check on Misty.

'Who is it? Who took my daughter?' Georgia asked, her voice tense, emotion all but blocking her words.

'We're working on that, Georgia,' Cross said. 'But this is the best close-up we could get of the person's face. Please, look and tell me if you recognize them.'

She walked backwards to get a better view of the smudged face on display on the screen. Justin stood close behind her; she could feel the heat of his body, and knew that if she needed to she could lean into his strength and he would stand strong.

The screenshot was a close-up of the person's face, side-on, seemingly from the point where they had looked up and down the corridor to check if anyone was there. It looked like a woman, but Georgia couldn't be sure. The long, dark hair partially covered the face. The picture was zoomed out and it looked like the person was wearing scrubs, but with the low lighting it was almost impossible to make out the color of the clothing.

'We've run the image through a few programs to see if we can get an idea of height, at the very least,' Cross explained. 'The person is approximately five foot five. We think it's a woman due to the slight build. We've compared the information we've got to staff files, and given what we know about the people you and Misty interacted with . . . ' He tailed off, and both Georgia and Justin turned to look at him.

'Who do you think it is?' Georgia prompted him.

'Given all the evidence, we've come up with Tracy Davidson.'

'How can you think it's Tracy? Why would she want to take Misty?'

'Is there any reason she might resent you coming back to town? Something to do with . . . ' Again Cross tailed off, but Georgia followed his line of vision. Justin fidgeted.

'Not that I can think of.' Georgia's eyes drifted back to the picture as she remembered something Tracy had said.

'Georgia, what are you thinking?' Justin stepped in front of her, and she pulled her thoughts back to the present.

'She said she'd seen the two of us together on Monday. That she used to see us around town and hoped she'd find someone like you.' She looked into

248

Justin's eyes to see what he made of it. She was aware of Jane moving restlessly in the background. The woman had yet to make a sound during the viewing of the CCTV. 'That's not enough to want to take someone's child, is it?'

'It's hard to tell,' Justin said. 'It depends on how that person measures someone else's relationship against their own experiences.' He was heading somewhere he shouldn't, but his gaze was asking Georgia if there was more, something she should be sharing.

She tried to look away, but he held her by the shoulders. 'If there's something more, then you need to tell us. What else did she say?'

Georgia didn't want to give up any more secrets, especially ones that weren't hers to surrender. She got the impression that Tracy hadn't told anyone else about her termination, and she didn't want to send the police off on the wrong track if Tracy had nothing to do with Misty's disappearance.

'This is our daughter, Georgia.

Nothing is more important that bringing her home.' Justin pulled her close and whispered in her ear, 'Don't hold out on me now, Georgia. If you want me to trust you, to believe everything you have told me, please don't lie about this.'

10

How could so much be unsaid, and yet every expectation, hope and desire from the past, in the present, and for the future be expressed so clearly in just a look? Georgia had to put herself in the line of fire right then if she wanted a father for Misty, and possibly a lifetime of love for herself. She had to choose between her loyalty to her family, in whatever form it would take, and her loyalty to a school girl who had grown up and moved on with her life. The harm that the secret could have done to Tracy back then had not lessened any now; it had the power to derail one or more people's lives. But what was more important — someone she used to know, or her own flesh and blood?

Cross sensed that Georgia needed some time. 'Jane, why don't you come fix some coffee for these folks, and we'll see if the doctor's done with his surgery. Georgia, you have the press conference in — ' He looked at his watch. ' — twenty-five minutes. I'll put a tail on Tracy Davidson for the time being. We don't have any actual proof that she's the abductor just now, so we'll sit tight and see what kind of reaction we get to the media coverage.'

Justin raised an eyebrow and nodded. Georgia had seen that look before between the two men, yesterday at the hospital. They knew something that they hadn't shared yet. As everyone apart from Justin and Georgia left the room, she took a deep breath and prepared herself for another difficult conversation.

'Is there anything else you need to tell me about Tracy?' Justin asked her. 'Something that might have relevance to what's going on now?'

She looked upwards quickly, for no reason other than that she knew it was what people did when they wanted forgiveness. *I'm sorry, Tracy. An* apology into the ether wasn't going to protect the young woman from any possible fallout from what Georgia was about to say, but it was time for her to look out for her own daughter.

'Tracy had a four-point-oh average in high school, in her junior year. She was going to apply to some good schools. Then over the course of a few months, her grades slipped and she started skipping classes.'

'This was nine years ago?'

'Yes. Her tutor asked me to speak to her. He had concerns about her health, but she refused to engage with him. It took me a few attempts, but one lunchtime she opened up.'

Justin waited quietly. Georgia knew how important this was, not just for Misty but for her and Justin too.

'She was pregnant, and scared. Her father was trying to further his political career at the time and she couldn't speak to him about it. So I answered her questions, gave her information, and set up an appointment at an advisory clinic in Jacksonville. She was undecided and wanted to speak to someone who didn't know her. I left town a couple of days before she was due to go.'

'You think she's after revenge?'

'No!' Georgia exclaimed, relieved he chose not to dwell on the last part of her sentence, but she didn't want him to get the wrong idea about Tracy. 'When I spoke with her on Monday night, I got the feeling she was comfortable with her decision.'

'So why the hesitation just now, when Cross asked you if you knew of any reason she might be involved?'

Georgia drew her lower lip between her teeth and laced her fingers together. She felt sick to her stomach, a hollow feeling that was gnawing at her. Had she shared Tracy's secret for no reason? Had she latched onto Tracy just because the policeman had named her as a possible suspect?

'I'm sorry, Justin. I think I've made a mistake. I don't think she meant anything by what she said.' The words fell from Georgia's mouth, panic rising in her throat. 'I don't want to get her into trouble. She's worked so hard to put the past behind her.'

Justin placed his hands on her shoulders, squeezing gently as he tried to catch her eye. She didn't want to meet his gaze and she looked everywhere, anywhere, other than at him.

'Calm down,' he said. 'Don't lose your train of thought. Forget for a second that this has to do with Misty. You helped Tracy before when she was in trouble. Think of this as helping her again. What if she's made a mistake, and she needs someone to help her put things right? No one's going to go and arrest her just on your say-so. Just tell me, in your own words, what she said to you.'

Georgia let go of the breath she'd been holding; it shuddered from her as if it was reluctant to leave, just as she was reluctant to speak. 'She said . . . ' Her eyes filled with tears. 'The last thing she said before she left was, 'Look after her while I'm gone.' '

Justin nodded, removed his hands from Georgia's shoulders, and turned away. She watched his movements like a hawk, trying to second-guess what he was thinking. He rubbed his hands over his face, blew out a breath, and clasped his hands at the back of his neck, his arms close to his head.

Georgia took a step toward him, just enough so she could reach out and touch his shoulder. He turned quickly and pulled her into his arms. They stood together in silence.

Jane came back into the room without knocking and noisily put down a tray on the desk. Georgia was conscious of the woman's eyes on Justin as he held her still.

'It's nearly ten o'clock. Are you ready?' Her words were for Georgia, but she looked at Justin.

'Yes, I am.'

'Are you joining the press conference, Justin?'

'No, he's not.' Georgia turned to face her, but did not have her attention.

'Jane.'

'Yes?'

Georgia finally had her attention. 'You said you'd be there with me. Justin has other things he needs to do, right?'

He nodded. 'You can do this, hun. It's about finding Misty, nothing else. I'm going to go see what I can find out.'

'I know. Will you come back later?' Georgia gave him a half-smile.

'You know it.' He held her face before kissing her. As he walked toward the door, he stopped in front of Jane. 'Take Georgia through the script. Don't let the press take control of this one. The bare minimum of information will be enough to start with.'

'I've done this before, Justin,' Jane snapped.

'Maybe so, but Misty is my daughter, and I don't want anything to go wrong. Understand me?'

* * *

Justin listened to the live press conference from his truck. He'd missed the first few minutes of it, as he'd stopped in to see Officer Cross. Officer Michaels had been tagged to trace Tracy Davidson, a mission which at first seemed relatively straightforward. A phone call to the hospital's HR department confirmed that her shift had started at ten, the same time as the press conference. Justin had followed the officer's cruiser at a distance to the hospital and waited in the parking lot while Michaels went in.

Although not involved in the case in any official capacity, Justin couldn't just sit around and wait for the officer to do his job. He wanted to find out more about Tracy, and thought first of Karen. Turning the radio down, he called through to Karen's office phone. He knew she'd been off sick yesterday with one of her migraines, but hoped she was back at work today. If his conversation with Paul was any indication of what she had to deal with, it was no wonder she'd prefer to hide away at home.

'Thank you for calling River Springs Police and Justice Department. This is Charlotte speaking. How may I help you?'

'Hi, this is Rose. I was hoping to speak to Karen.'

'I'm sorry, boss, she's still out sick. Did you want to talk to anyone else?'

'No, that's okay. Thanks.'

'Sure, boss.'

Michaels returned to his vehicle and pulled out of the parking lot. Justin continued to follow him to Mayor Davidson's residence, where Tracy's older model SUV was parked in the driveway. Obviously something hadn't gone according to plan, as she was supposed to be at work. Michaels drove past, turned around further up the street, and parked a discreet distance away. Justin knew the procedure: the officer would sit and wait for as long as it took, whether that was minutes or hours.

After just a short while Tracy left the home she shared with her father, Mayor Davidson, driving toward town. She visited a private house in one of the more expensive neighborhoods, carrying a large black bag as she left her car. After half an hour she left, driving next to a retirement village where she spent approximately forty minutes. Justin followed the officer, who followed Tracy to three other private residences over the next few hours, and each time she took in the black bag.

It became obvious, after she stopped off for supplies at the drugstore, that she was providing medical care to people, secondary to her job at the hospital. Justin fought hard not to get out the car each time she did, so he could challenge her about Misty's disappearance, but he knew that he would jeopardize the case and also her safety. He should back off, go find Georgia, and let the sheriff's department get on with the investigating. He should.

His cell bleeped. A text message from Paul: *Justin, I'm sorry.*

And another: *I didn't mean to do it.*

What was wrong with him? There was only one way to find out. Justin cast a quick glance through the window to make sure the officer was still on duty, put his truck in gear, and swung out into the traffic. Paul had some explaining to do.

★   ★   ★

'Good job, Georgia.' Cross escorted her into his office, closing the door behind her. 'How are you feeling?'

Georgia held her hands out in front of her. She was shaking.

'It's a natural reaction,' Jane said. Georgia smiled, relieved that Jane had returned to her previous pleasant self after Justin had spoken to her. 'You were very dignified.'

'I just want my daughter back, Jane. I'll do whatever it takes.'

'Let me update you on what's been

happening,' said Cross. 'We interviewed the doctor you saw on the CCTV. He reluctantly corroborated the nurse's statement, but asked that he not be identified as part of the investigation when we've ruled him out.'

'Do you still need me to ID him and the nurse?'

'Not at this stage. CCTV from another department shows the doctor making his rounds throughout the night and the nurse leaving the building when her shift ended. Staff have to clock in at the start of their shift when they enter through the staff entrance. They also clock out and leave through the same door.'

'You still think that the person on the tape is Tracy?'

'Tracy clocked in for her shift at nine forty-five a.m. on Monday morning. She clocked out at nine twenty-five p.m. that evening.'

'Just after she left me.'

'Records show she clocked in again at nine fifty-five.'

'Ready for her shift on Tuesday?'

'The same evening.'

Georgia closed her eyes briefly.

'Tracy didn't show up to work today, after her rest day. Michaels followed her as she visited some private residences. We're going to invite her to the station to answer some questions about her movements after she left the hospital on Monday night and to ascertain what she did on her day off yesterday.'

'I don't need to be here, do I?'

'No. In fact, you've had a busy morning. It might be an idea to go get some lunch and take a break. Jane will take you home, won't you?'

'To Justin's house first,' Georgia said. Jane held the door open, waiting for Georgia to follow. 'You'll let me know if anything . . . ' She didn't finish her sentence, leaving the words unspoken.

'Of course,' Jane said reassuringly.

Georgia exchanged a look with the sheriff, who nodded at her with a smile. 'Of course,' he said.

★ ★ ★

Justin stopped by Paul's office but there was no one there. He crossed the road to check Charlie's bar and the motel, but neither proprietor had seen him since yesterday. Paul's home was only a few streets over, so Justin, stiff from sitting in the truck for several hours, decided to walk there.

The curtains were drawn downstairs, in keeping with Karen's normal routine when she had a migraine. Justin couldn't remember her having one in recent months, but maybe Paul's behavior over the last few days had triggered this occasion. He knocked on the door gently, not wanting to wake her if she was sleeping, but the door opened quickly, only a few inches. It was Karen.

'Justin, what are you doing here?'

'Hi, Karen. I'm looking for Paul. He sent me a strange text. I just wanted to check on him.' Justin noted her hair was pulled back from her face, unusual for her.

'He's not here. I kicked his butt out on Monday.'

'And how are you? Can I come in, catch up? I'm worried about P.' He put a hand on the doorframe. Karen's head turned slightly toward the inside of the house and she shifted her weight from one foot to the other, matching Justin's body language as he leaned casually.

'I can't shake this migraine, Justin. The house is a mess. I haven't had the energy to do anything. Maybe another time?' She gave an over-bright smile and started to close the door.

'And Paul?'

'I have more important things to worry about right now. I'll be back at work as soon as I can. Thanks for stopping by.'

He didn't move, and Karen hesitated as a car pulled up outside. Justin followed her gaze and heard her emit a tiny gasp.

Tracy exited her car and walked up

the path, black bag in hand. 'Hi, Detective Rose,' she called brightly, swallowing rapidly as she neared.

'Ms. Davidson.' Justin nodded politely. He watched as Michaels's cruiser pulled up down the road. 'I didn't know you two knew each other.'

'I'm just checking up on Mrs. Denali. She asked me to stop by. I understand she needs some medication.' Tracy reached into her bag and pulled out a bottle of pills, which she rattled.

'Okay. Well, I'll get off,' Justin said. 'I still need to catch up with Paul.' Tracy's smile faltered at mention of his name but Justin didn't react, looking over his shoulder only as he reached the pavement.

Karen had opened the door enough to usher Tracy in, and then firmly slammed it closed. Justin walked to his truck and looked pointedly at the officer before getting into the cab.

Now was the time to ask Tracy Davidson some questions, Justin thought as he drove slowly away.

'The boss's truck isn't here.' Jane pulled the car to a halt outside the property. 'He's obviously got other things to do.'

Georgia ignored the barb. 'I'll wait. It's nice and peaceful here.' She could see from the woman's frown that she didn't understand. 'There's nothing of Misty's here, Jane. Everywhere I look at home, something reminds me that she's not there.'

Jane didn't reply to that, and Georgia thanked her for the ride. 'I'll call you if anything changes,' Georgia told her.

Jane drove off at speed as Georgia walked up the path toward the front of the house. She didn't have a key, and if Justin no longer hid his spare in the same place she'd be quite happy sitting out on the porch. The house had once been her home, and she'd missed it very much in the first months after she'd left, when all she could afford were cramped studio apartments. She let herself through the gate to the back yard and crossed to the side, reaching her hand into a hole in an old, gnarled tree. That was where the spare key was kept when she lived there, but there was nothing in her hand when she pulled it out but leaf mold. Some things had changed, then. She smiled ruefully.

Georgia rounded the house and started up the porch steps, then stopped. The screen door hung off its hinges and a large pane of glass was broken, a jacket stuffed around the edges of the hole, no doubt to protect the arm of whoever had reached inside to turn the key. She reached for her cell phone and dialed the number for the station. If Justin was at work, they could put her through. She didn't want to go into the house; it was a crime scene and he would want to deal with the break-in.

'Good morning, thank you for calling — '

Georgia interrupted the woman on the other end. 'Hi, this is Georgia Baxter. I need to speak to Rose as a matter of urgency, please.'

'One moment, I'll try his line.' There was silence. 'His phone is diverted to his cell, ma'am. Can I connect you?'

'Please.'

There was a brief delay, then Justin's voice came on the line. 'Hey, hun. How are you? Charlotte said you needed to speak to me,' he said softly.

'Justin, you need to come home. There's been a break-in.'

'At your house? Are you okay?' Georgia heard some movement and a muffled curse. 'I dropped the phone. Let me just pull over.'

'I'm at your house. I had Jane drive me here after the press conference. Where are you? Can you come now?'

'I'll be five minutes. Don't touch anything, hun,' he said, and cut the connection.

Several long minutes later, Georgia heard the roar of Justin's truck and the squeal of brakes as he came to a stop outside. 'Georgia?'

'In back,' she called and he strode

toward her, his gaze only on her.

'Are you okay? Did you disturb anyone?' He hugged her close. He hadn't even glanced at the house, and Georgia marveled again at how safe she felt in his strong embrace.

She pushed away from him slightly and looked from his face to the back porch. 'No, I just called you straightaway. Oh, I hope this has nothing to do with me . . . '

'Let me go look.'

'Be careful, Justin. Whoever broke in might still be in there.'

'Then they'll wish they broke into someone else's house, won't they?'

* * *

Justin pushed open the back door with his elbow, stepping carefully over the broken glass on the floor. The jacket covering the shards in the broken pane fell out. It was a navy-blue anorak, nondescript apart from the hip flask sticking out of the pocket. Justin knew who it belonged to before he pulled an evidence bag from his own pocket. Covering his hand with it, he picked the silver flask up. He had one just like it in the back of a cupboard somewhere. The owner's initials would be engraved on the back; where Justin's had JR, this one had PD.

Leaving the flask on the counter, Justin quickly scoped the kitchen for any other signs of damage to his property or injury to the housebreaker. There were none; Paul knew how to break into a place without injuring himself, no matter how drunk he was. Expecting to find Paul asleep in one of the bedrooms, Justin headed along the hallway and up the stairs, freezing when he hit the first landing where there the staircase turned to the right. To the left, up two steps, was a door leading to his office. When he had left the house last night, and every time he was not in the office, the door was padlocked. He kept his gun collection in there and he'd learned from his father and his grandfather never to leave the room open, just in case.

The door was wide open, but not because it had been busted open. The padlock hung from the latch, obviously jimmied. There was no damage to either the lock or the door. As he stepped quietly through the doorway, Justin's first concern was for the gun cupboard, but it was still locked. Paul might be an idiot, but even he knew better than to mess with Justin's guns.

A glance to the far side of the room told him that Paul was passed out on the leather sofa. There were several half-empty bottles on the floor, as well as a cell phone and photo frames. Justin crossed the wooden floorboards silently, knowing from experience which ones creaked and groaned under a man's weight. He squatted by the sofa and picked up one of the framed photos. It was of him and Georgia at a barbecue. Neither of them were great at posing for a picture, but this one reminded him of how good they were together.

They smiled at each other in the photo; they'd just shared a joke. Whoever the photographer was had captured Georgia at her best, relaxed and happy. Justin had kept it for sentimental reasons, and during those nights that he missed her more than anything else, he used to lie on the sofa and fall asleep with the photo beside him.

Paul snored and mumbled something in his sleep, his arms crossed over an object on his chest like he was cuddling something close. Justin carefully prized it from under Paul's arms. It was a photo of the two of them the day they graduated from the police academy. They'd had such high hopes that day, jubilant to have passed, and excited about protecting their home town from the bad guys. The party that followed on graduation night was one of many. Justin should have noticed earlier that Paul liked his booze, until it got to the point that it affected his day job, and by then the rot had already set in. Paul had been angry when the force retired him, way too early in his opinion. He'd been angry at Justin, at his colleagues, at every damn person but himself.

'P,' Justin whispered, 'how did it come to this?'

With a loud snore, Paul woke up. He yawned, his mouth a gaping hole in his face, and Justin turned his face away from the smell of alcohol that accompanied the yawn.

'Hey bro, you made it.' Paul pushed himself up on his elbows.

'I see you had a party at my expense.'

'Yeah, sorry about the booze. I'll replace it.'

'What about the house?'

'Huh?' Paul frowned. 'Oh, damn. I broke the door. The spare key wasn't there, man. What was I supposed to do?'

Justin remembered he'd given that damn key to Jane when he'd been seeing her earlier in the year. He hadn't asked for it back. 'And my office?' he said.

Paul swung his legs to the floor as he

sat up, his eyes struggling to focus. 'Tricks of the trade, my friend.' He grinned, wiggling a set of lock picks that he found under his leg. 'Wouldn't be much of a private detective, would I, if I couldn't break in.'

'It was locked for a reason, Paul. My office is private.' Justin tried hard to stay calm, but frustration at his friend's lack of respect was starting to build.

'You and Karen both. 'It's my room; stay out of it. I need my own space, Paul. You're not the only one who can keep secrets, you know.' ' Paul's expression soured as he mimicked his wife in a high-pitched voice. 'You've got a stupid gun collection and she's got a stupid doll collection. Well, I'm starting my own collection.' He lurched forward suddenly, his hand fishing for one of the bottles on the floor.

Justin caught him and pushed him gently back against the sofa. Paul had found what he was looking for. 'I'm starting an empty bottle collection,' he announced, chuckling away to himself.

'You need help, P. You can't go on like this.'

'Help? From who? My wife is too busy with work, her support group, and her dolls. You?' Paul leaned forward, pointing a finger at Justin's chest, his voice getting louder. 'You're too busy making boss and pining after some woman who left you years ago. Who's going to help me, Justin? Tell me!'

Justin sat back onto the floor, such was the viciousness of Paul's tone. 'What was that text about, P? 'I'm sorry. I didn't mean to.' What didn't you mean to do?' Justin kept his voice low.

'Hell if I know, man. Just apply it to anything I've done, or store it for anything I mess up in the future.'

'Did you find anything out about Tracy?'

'Who?'

'Mayor Davidson's daughter.'

'What?'

Justin thought he was losing Paul; his eyes were unfocused and his words ran together. His behavior when he drank became erratic. This was how he had been when things had gotten really bad, just after he was taken off active duty. Just before he was retired out. 'P, yesterday you said you were going to see what you could dig out about her.'

Paul laughed, barely able to keep his eyes open. 'Know what?'

'What?' Justin ran a hand across his jaw. 'What do you know?'

'She's a great lay.' Paul's head nodded until his chin rested on his chest. He was out cold.

Justin let out a sigh, and then turned, hearing the creak of a floorboard behind him.

'I came to see what was taking you so long.' Georgia leaned against the desk, distaste at the sight of Paul evident. Her nose wrinkled as she spoke. 'You heard that?'

'I did. You told me he had an affair.'

'Yes. He was the one who got Tracy pregnant.'

Justin turned on the floor to face

Georgia and moved on his knees towards her. He wrapped his arms around her waist. He wished that he could turn the clock back all those years to the night when she had left; that she had trusted him enough to come to him when all this had been happening. But he couldn't go back; he couldn't change what had happened. He could only deal with the here and now.

'How did we get here, hun? How did it come to this?' he whispered against her midriff. She was silent, only pressing her hands to his head. The answers were there, among the history, the secrets and lies; they just had to work through all the mess together. He had to trust her, because so far what she had told him was true. And that made everyone else a liar.

11

Justin had sworn loudly as he finished on the phone to Karen, causing Georgia to look up from making coffee. He'd called Karen to come get her husband, and she'd flatly refused to do so; had said that he wasn't her problem, and that he shouldn't be Justin's either. Then she'd hung up.

'What are you going to do?' Georgia asked him.

Justin paced as she stirred his drink. 'He needs looking after, but I'll be damned if it's going to be me this time. We've got enough to worry about without Paul.' His cell rang and his dour expression lifted momentarily, thinking it was Karen calling back. 'Oh, hi, Cross.'

Georgia stepped around the counter with his coffee and watched him, holding her breath.

'Yes, Georgia's with me. Did you talk to Tracy?'

Georgia wished he would put it on speaker so that she could hear, but she only got one side of the conversation.

'Okay. She did? Sure, yes, we can come down. Now?' He took the coffee from Georgia and shrugged apologetically at her. 'Give me fifteen minutes. I have something I need to quickly take care of, and then we'll be with you. Bye.'

'Well? What did he say?' Georgia took the mug from him just as he was about to take a sip.

'He wants to show us Tracy's interview. She's been sedated by a nurse because she got very upset. Cross is calling her father.'

'Poor Tracy,' Georgia whispered.

'Hey, this is about Misty.'

'You don't have to keep reminding me.'

'I do, because you're too worried about the woman who's kidnapped our daughter.'

'You don't know she's involved, Justin.'

'We won't find out by arguing.'

Georgia stared at him, wanting to tell him he was wrong about Tracy, but unable to put it into words. She knew Tracy; he didn't. Just like she knew her daughter and he didn't. Did he have the right to be this involved?

Her eyes widened as the thought registered. Where had that come from? He was watching her, looking through her, his eyes narrowing. She knew it was too good to be true. She'd wondered how he'd gone from not wanting to know anything to wanting to know everything. Because it felt so good — because she needed someone to help her through — she'd lapped up his attention. And despite his words and his whispered assurances that he believed her, Georgia still felt there was something holding him back.

'Justin, I — '

'Well, well, if it ain't Sexy Sweets. You two lovebirds having a little fight?' Paul drawled as he staggered into the room, crashing into a chair. Georgia shivered, his voice making her skin crawl.

'Back off, Paul.' Justin's voice was low.

'Ah, don't be like that, bro. You forget, I've been there too. I know how feisty she can be.'

Georgia closed her eyes against Justin's glare. There would always be Paul between them. He'd been there before Georgia had set foot in town, and he was there after she'd left. They'd been friends since high school, and that bond ran deeper than anything else in Justin's life. His one constant. She'd never win.

'Nothing to say, Sweets?'

'Not to you.'

'Too busy using those lovely lips kissing up to the man you cheated on, ain't ya?'

'Paul, that's enough.' Justin stepped around Georgia and put a hand on his best friend's chest to stop him moving closer. She turned to look, and Paul's sneer sent a shiver through her.

'You're right, it's enough. Everything went wrong when she showed up, Justin. I keep telling you, she's trouble.'

'How am I trouble, Paul?' Georgia rounded on him angrily. 'What have I ever done to you? Anything that's gone wrong in your life is of your own making.'

'Bullshit. You tried to ruin my friendship; my marriage.'

'Your marriage was on the way out when you slept with Tracy. I should have gone and told Karen that night, rather than leaving. I should have let everyone see what you really are.' Georgia moved forward, but Justin grasped her upper arm like a parent holding two arguing kids apart.

'Karen knows all about the other women. She drove me to sleep around. She only wanted to have sex when she was ovulating. She's only ever been about having a baby.' Paul's tone was bitter, as if he hated the taste of the words he spoke.

'Women?' Justin asked, his eyebrows raised in surprise.

'Sure.' Paul focused on Justin, a smile curving his lips. 'Sexy Sweets there wasn't the first.' He laughed. 'Hell, she wasn't even the best. You could do a whole lot better, bro.'

'I never — ' Georgia started to shout, but Justin released his hold on her arm and swung his fist at Paul's jaw, knocking him backwards into the doorframe.

'Justin!' Georgia gasped.

'I've had enough of his mouth.' He rubbed his knuckles, looking at the unconscious man on the floor, then bent down to hook his hands under Paul's arms. 'We've got to get to the station. I'm not leaving him here. Help me get him into the truck.'

Georgia stood still, her mouth open. After what Paul had just said, Justin still wanted to take care of him. Unbelievable. Silently she grabbed Paul's ankles and together they made their way out to Justin's car, manhandling him into the front seat because he was too cumbersome to fold into the bench seat.

'You'll have to hop in the back,' Justin told her. 'I'm just going to call Michaels and have him come over with a locksmith to get this place secure.'

Georgia glowered in the truck while she watched Justin talk on his cell. Paul snored in the front. As far as she was concerned, everything that had happened was because of Justin's best friend. If he only he hadn't come over that night. If only he hadn't attacked her. If only she hadn't left. She and Justin and Misty could have been a proper family. She should have been able to trust that Justin loved her enough to take her word over Paul's. But even back then there must have been something missing, something in the back of her mind that told her he would never choose her over his best friend. That was why she'd left.

'You okay?' Justin asked her as he got in and started the engine, catching her gaze in the rear-view mirror.

With her lips clamped together, Georgia nodded and fixed her attention out of the window. She heard Justin sigh as they pulled out. As they drove into town, only Paul's grunts and snores punctuated the frosty silence. The wall of ice between herself and Justin that had started to thaw on Monday after the bus accident was freezing right back over.

* * *

At the sheriff's department they left Paul in the truck, still out cold, and walked side by side but far apart into the ops room, where Officer Cross and Jane waited for them.

'What have you got?' Justin's question was curt, but only Georgia seemed to notice. Officer Cross précised the interview for them.

'Just to give you a context in which to watch the tape,' he said, 'Tracy came in and willingly talked to us. She was calm while we asked general questions about her routines and her health. We pulled her medical records, and it seems she's been receiving regular counselling for mental health issues since she was seventeen. She was taking medication until a few years ago, but seemed to be doing well without it.'

'She mentioned that she'd had a few issues when we spoke on Monday,' Georgia said.

'And she spoke very warmly about seeing you again. She said you were a great help to her when she had a hard time in high school. I asked her what she meant, and she admitted to becoming pregnant and having a termination.'

Georgia nodded. She could feel Justin's gaze on her, but she chose not to look at him.

'I showed her the CCTV tape, the one you saw this morning. She was still quite relaxed at this point, confident that it wasn't her on the tape. But when I questioned her about her movements earlier on Monday, she became uncomfortable. Michaels, play the tape.'

Georgia focused her attention on the screen, glancing for a second at Justin, who sat with his legs crossed and his arms folded, his expression dark. Tracy appeared on the screen, a close-up of her face. Cross started to question her.

'Tell me about Monday morning, Tracy,' he said on the tape. 'You were due to be at work?'

'Sure. Daddy was giving me a lift to work; my shift started at ten. Just as we were leaving the house, Daddy got a call from his office to say there'd been an accident. Some little kids were trapped in a bus. As the scene of the accident was on the way to the hospital, Daddy wanted to stop by to see what was happening.'

'Did you go with him?'

'Naturally. As a nurse, I thought I might be able to help if necessary. But everything seemed to be under control.'

'How did you know that?'

'Daddy and I went to the command center. The person coordinating said everything was taken care of; that the police and fire departments were on the scene and working together to get the children to safety.'

'And who was it you spoke to?'

'Mrs. Denali.' Tracy looked scared as she spoke, her eyes flitting from left to right several times as if checking who was in the room.

The tape was paused as Cross said, 'Watch how her demeanor changes. You know we picked her up at the Denali residence, right?'

Georgia looked at Justin as he nodded. 'Yeah, she turned up to see Karen just as I was leaving,' he said. 'She said she had some medication for her.'

'You didn't think to tell me this?' Georgia asked.

'There were other things that needed taking care of, Georgia,' Justin snapped.

'When we searched the medicine bag she had with her when we picked her up,' Cross said, 'there were basic medical supplies — dressings, bandages, and so on.'

'She does medical visits, right?' Justin asked.

'Yes. She told me that straight off the bat. She supplements her income by visiting old folks who can't afford to pay for medical care. When I asked why she'd phoned in sick today rather than go to work, she admitted that there were more people than normal who needed her help.'

Cross took a piece of paper from the desk in front of him and looked at Georgia. 'We have your toxicological report back, Georgia. The lab found traces of chloral hydrate in your blood. It's used as a sedative, often in liquid form.'

'So I was drugged?'

He nodded. 'There were some prescribed pain medications in Tracy's bag also, and some prefilled syringes of a clear liquid. The techs are just testing those now, but Tracy corroborated some of the facts. Here.'

The tape restarted.

'You seem nervous mentioning Mrs.

Denali,' Cross said to Tracy. 'Do you know her?'

'A little, yes, sir,' Tracy replied.

'You get along with her?'

There was a pause before Tracy answered, looking at her hands on the table in front of her. 'Not so much.'

'What were you doing at her house today?'

'She needed some medication.'

'For her migraine?'

'Yes.'

'She couldn't get her own medication?'

'She'd used it all, sir. Couldn't leave the house to get any more.'

'How did she know you offer the service you do?'

'I guess someone told her.'

The tape was paused again.

'I couldn't figure out the relationship between Tracy and Karen Denali at this point,' Cross explained to Georgia, 'so I changed tack and asked about her visit with you in Misty's room on Monday night. Tracy's body language changed again at this point. She became more positive; sat up straight and maintained eye contact. She talked about Misty like she'd met her on more than one occasion.'

'But she only spent twenty minutes or so with me, and Misty was under sedation still.'

'She told me that Misty has a soft toy she liked, but that she likes dolls more; that she has lots of dolls. When my team searched your house, Georgia, I don't remember seeing many toys around Misty's room, just a — '

'Ragdoll on her bed,' Georgia finished the sentence. 'Misty hasn't played with her dolls in about a year. In fact, when we moved to River Springs, she gave them all away to Goodwill, and she only brought her ragdoll with her.'

'I went through the timings of her day at work, Monday, then.' Cross nodded to Michaels, who forwarded the tape.

'You clocked in at nine forty-five a.m.,' Cross continued to Tracy. 'You clocked out for your break at two-thirty p.m.' Tracy nodded. 'What did you do at lunch?'

'I brought my lunch from home. I sat out in the park and made some phone calls.'

'Then you clocked back in at three twenty-nine p.m. and out at nine twenty-five p.m. But your shift ended at eight p.m., didn't it?'

'I did a little overtime, then I visited with Ms. Baxter.'

'You left after your visit?'

'Yes, sir.'

'Where did you go?'

'Home, sir.'

'Your clocking card shows you came back into to work at nine fifty-five p.m.'

'No, sir. I went home.'

'How can that be, Tracy?'

'I don't know, Sheriff. I visited with Ms. Baxter, and then I went home.'

'Can anyone verify this? Was your father home?'

'No, sir. He was at a rally.'

'And did he see you later that night,

when he came home?'

'I went to bed at about ten-thirty. I didn't see him until the next morning.'

'And what time was that?'

'I woke later than usual. It'd been a busy day on Monday.'

Tracy's fidgeting became worse. She licked her lips repeatedly, like she was thirsty, despite there being a jug of water on the table in front of her.

'Nothing to do you with you being at the hospital all night?'

'No, sir.'

'Let's have a look at the CCTV footage again, shall we?'

The tape paused, frozen on Tracy's pale face. Cross again addressed Georgia. 'It was from this point that she became increasingly anxious. She remained adamant that she'd gone home and that it wasn't her on the tape.'

'So how can you prove it was or wasn't her?' Georgia asked. Justin was broodingly silent, his eyes fixed on the large screen, concentrating hard, despite all of the other smaller CCTV screens displaying a myriad of different images.

'We checked the CCTV from the parking lot. Tracy left the building, got in her car, and drove off. Her car never returned to the parking lot.'

'So she was telling the truth? It wasn't her?' Georgia flashed a triumphant look in Justin's direction, but he didn't respond. He seemed to be concentrating on one of the smaller screens.

'To a certain extent. Officer Michaels asked Tracy what her route home was, which included stopping for gas, and pulled up any CCTV footage he could find. Footage from inside the gas station showed her browsing for a magazine and having a conversation with another customer.'

'Who?' Justin asked gruffly.

'We're not sure. Someone of a similar height and build, with blond hair under a cap. They kept their back to the camera. The conversation lasted about a minute, and then Tracy paid for her gas and the other person left on foot, without buying anything. Michaels was unable to trace the other person on CCTV.'

'You think Tracy was working with someone else?' Justin asked.

'You tell me.' Cross indicated to the large screen. Officer Michaels had moved the tape forward ten minutes.

Tracy's face had crumpled. There were tears on her cheeks, and her eyes were full of fear.

'Do you have Misty Baxter?' Cross asked her. 'Where are you keeping her?'

'No, no. I wouldn't hurt her. I wouldn't hurt her. I would take care of her.'

'What do you mean, Tracy, take care of her? Do you know where she is?'

'My job is to take care of her. Not to hurt her. She took care of me. It's my turn to take care of her.' Tracy began to rock in her seat.

'Tracy, who took care of you? Who's taking care of Misty?'

'She was sleeping. Sleeping with her

dollies. Sound asleep.'

'Who was sleeping? Where is Misty?'

'She said she would tell on me. Tell my daddy what I'd done. She said I'd been a naughty girl.'

'Tracy, focus. Who are you talking about? Who's going to tell on you?'

'Daddy would be angry at me. I can't let him know. He'd be in big trouble. They wouldn't let him be mayor anymore.'

Georgia found it hard to watch as Tracy became more and more distraught, saying she was sorry, begging for her daddy.

The tape stopped there, and Georgia took a deep breath as she listened to Cross.

'I stopped the interview at that point,' he said. 'I got the station doctor to sedate her. She's under observation in the medical bay and her father's on the way.'

'I think he's already here,' Justin said, standing quickly and heading for the door.

'Justin!' Georgia called after him, and Cross drew her attention to the CCTV screen that Justin had been so preoccupied with. Images from the parking lot showed Paul lolling against the truck, jabbing his finger at another man.

* * *

Justin covered the distance from the station exit to his truck at a run and grabbed Paul by the collar, pulling him away from the older man he was toe to toe with.

'That's right, Detective Rose, call your buddy off.'

'Mayor Davidson,' Justin said, pushing Paul back against the truck, 'what's this about?'

'I was just filling the good mayor here in on his lovely daughter,' Paul sniggered, the fumes on his breath causing Justin to turn his head away.

'This drunk is maligning my daughter's reputation, and I won't stand for it.' The mayor pointed at Paul. 'He shouldn't be allowed out in public in this state.'

'She came looking for it, Mr. Mayor,' Paul slurred.

'Paul, that's enough,' Justin hissed.

'Yes, it is. More than enough.' The mayor straightened his tie and swiped his hand over his silver hair.

'Your daughter is waiting for you inside, Mr. Mayor.' Justin met the older man's stare.

Paul hooted. 'Nice one, Justin, very funny. Your daughter is locked up, Mr. Mayor, just like she was knocked up.'

'Detective Rose, control your friend. If he continues to cast aspersions on my family, I will take legal action.'

'Is anything he said untrue, Mayor Davidson?' Justin challenged him.

The mayor looked shaken, but ever the politician, he stood tall and faced Justin. The two men's eyes locked. Then Paul threw up over the mayor's shoes. Justin helped his friend over to a low wall edging the parking lot, crouching down to hold Paul's head between his knees.

'Waste of space,' the mayor said disdainfully. 'I'm glad this man is no longer on the police force. He's a disgrace to the badge. I'm only sorry it took me so long to get him out.'

Justin registered his words and stood slowly, turning to stare at him. 'I'm sorry, sir; I don't think I heard you correctly.'

'Oh, you did. Your predecessor, Donovan, and I had a good working relationship, and you'd do well to foster the same. I have friends in every place imaginable. So when I find out, admittedly several years down the line, that my seventeen-year-old daughter has had a termination because she'd become pregnant by some no-good cop — '

'You took care of it.' Justin finished the sentence for him, taking several steps towards the mayor.

'You wouldn't do the same, Rose?' He straightened his back and turned squarely to face Justin. 'I understand you've recently discovered you're a father, and your child is missing.'

Justin swallowed against the thick ball of emotion that suddenly developed in his throat. He clenched his teeth together, breathing through his nose to control the anger that was building.

'Well, wouldn't you do everything in your power to do right by your family?' As Justin walked away, the mayor's smooth voice jarred over the jagged peaks in his conscience.

Justin glanced from the mayor's back to the back of Paul's head as he choked up bile onto the pavement. With both his parents gone, Justin had had to find his own family, in the form of his best friend. When he'd started his relationship with Georgia, he'd thought that she was going to be his family too. After she'd left him, Paul was all he had left; so why wouldn't Justin look out for him and take care of him when things got tough? The mayor was right, that was what family meant. But he couldn't seem to get the balance right between Paul and Georgia, and now Misty.

⋆ ⋆ ⋆

As the door closed behind Justin, another door in Georgia's heart closed too. She knew he was running to Paul's side yet again.

'Can I please see Tracy?' she asked Cross.

He shook his head. 'I don't think that's a good idea, Georgia. You saw how distraught she was on the tape.'

'She's been sedated for a while, right? She'll have calmed down now. Maybe I can just sit with her and see if she talks to me.' Georgia felt tears in her eyes and breathed deeply to try to control them. 'Please?'

Cross nodded and took her down to the medical bay. After a brief discussion, the duty doctor showed her to a chair. Michaels was perched on the corner of a desk nearby. Tracy lay on a gurney and turned her head, smiling, when she saw Georgia.

'Hi, Tracy.'

'Hi, Ms. Baxter.'

'Georgia, please. Remember, we're not at school now. How are you feeling?'

Tracy rolled over onto her side to face Georgia, who took her hand. 'I'm good. Are you here to ask me some questions, too?' She looked sad, and Georgia forced a smile, knowing that she had to ask her.

'Well, let's see. What's your favorite color?'

The younger woman laughed. 'Yellow. What's yours?'

'I like red.'

'What's Misty's favorite color?' Tracy sobered, her brown eyes serious.

'She likes yellow too. She has a ragdoll dressed all in yellow. She says it reminds her of the sunshine.'

'Misty likes dolls, huh?'

'She does. But her ragdoll is at home, alone.'

'Oh, Misty won't like that. But she

has lots of other dolls where she's sleeping.'

'That's great. She doesn't like to be alone.' Georgia's breath stuck in her throat. Tracy did know where she was.

'She's not alone.'

'She isn't?' Georgia tipped her head to the side to look at Tracy closely.

'No. She has her own room, with lots of dolls.' Tracy sat up, swinging her legs over the side of the gurney. She leaned forward and took Georgia's other hand. 'And I've been helping take care of her. Making sure she takes her medicine.'

'Isn't she a lucky girl? Does that make you feel good, to look after her?'

'Sure. It's kind of like having my own daughter.'

'But she's not your daughter, is she, Tracy?'

'No.' Tracy's head dropped slightly, her mouth turning down. 'She's yours.'

'And Justin Rose's,' Georgia prompted, remembering how Tracy had hoped to find a man like Justin.

'No.' Tracy frowned and shook her

head. 'No. That's not right.'

'I'm sorry. What's not right?'

'I terminated the other baby that should have been hers. You took his baby with you when you left, and you didn't tell anyone. That baby should have been hers too.'

'Whose baby, Tracy?' Georgia thought she already knew, but needed to hear Tracy say it.

'She made me help take Misty. She said as I had slept with her husband, and then killed his baby, it was only fair I help her. She said she'd tell my daddy, and then he wouldn't be mayor anymore.'

'It was a long time ago. It wouldn't stop your daddy from being mayor.'

'She told me you slept with her husband too, and if she wasn't able to have her own kids, at least she could have one baby that belonged to her man. I'm glad you got to have your baby.'

'Oh, Tracy. You were young and you went through it alone.' Georgia stood and put her arms around her. The young woman held herself so still, she was so tense. 'It's okay, honey. It's going to be okay.'

Tracy let out a juddering sigh, and Georgia felt her relax.

'Can you tell me where Misty is, Tracy? Help me find my daughter.'

'My daddy will still be mayor?' Tracy asked in a little-girl voice.

'Yes.' Georgia closed her eyes and held her breath.

'She's in Karen's baby room. She's with the other babies.'

Georgia left Tracy with a hug. She headed out to where Justin stood, planning as she moved. Justin knew the address, and if they took Paul with them, it would give her an excuse to get into the house.

When she reached the truck, Justin was just helping Paul into the back. He looked rough. His shirt was soiled with vomit and he smelled awful. She waited until Justin had straightened up.

'Let's take him home,' she said.

Justin looked at her questioningly. 'You're going to play nice now?'

'Sure, Justin. Let's go make believe that none of this is happening. Let's go to Karen and Paul's house and pretend that he's not a down-and-out drunk, and that she's not a child-stealing witch.'

'What the hell?' Justin slammed the rear passenger door.

'You heard. Apparently Karen blackmailed Tracy into helping her take Misty, as payback for sleeping with her husband.'

'You or Tracy?'

Georgia ignored the barb for now. 'Karen threatened to tell Mayor Davidson all about Tracy's termination so that he wouldn't be re-elected next week. Tracy never told her father about being pregnant; she's kept it a secret all these years.'

'He knows.'

'What?'

'I said the mayor knows. He found out about it, and had my boss throw

Paul out of the force.'

Georgia laughed. 'Oh, believe me, Mayor Davidson wouldn't have been the only person to have reason to get rid of Paul.'

'Meaning?'

'When sleeping beauty there sobers up, ask him whose fault it was that you were under investigation for the deaths of those two officers on your watch. Ask him to tell you honestly where he was when those carjackers were shooting at your colleagues. Ask him why he was hiding around the corner, ignoring their calls for help, while he kept swigging from the hip flask he carried with him everywhere. Ask him why he didn't return fire at the assailants. Ask him to tell you it all, in as much detail as he told me the night I left.'

'What do you know? You weren't here for nearly a decade. You should keep your opinions to yourself. I'm sick of hearing the lies you tell about people I care for.'

'And I've had it with you taking his

side, and now Karen's. According to Karen, because she can't have children of her own, she thinks it's only right to take one that her husband apparently fathered. Well, I didn't sleep with Paul, and she has no right to my daughter.' Georgia poked Justin in the chest, hard. 'Whether you believe me or not, Justin, you and I made a baby. It's up to you if you choose to be more than a biological father to her. I want you to drive me to his house so that I can get my little girl.'

She pulled open the door, climbed into the cab, put on her safety belt, and wound down the window. 'Now.'

* * *

Justin held on to Paul as Georgia pounded on the door. She stood to one side so that Karen wouldn't see her when she answered.

'Justin, what are you doing?' Karen cracked the door and then saw who Justin was holding. 'Oh. I told you, I don't want him back.'

'I don't care, Karen. He's your husband, for better or for worse. I'm bringing him in.'

'But — '

Georgia stepped forward then, with a fake smile, and pushed the door open. Karen staggered back in shock as Georgia walked into the darkened hallway.

'What are you doing here?' Karen asked.

Georgia continued to smile. 'I just wanted to come and see that you were okay. What with everything that's been going on.' She paused, looking for the other woman's reaction, and saw only contempt.

'I'm doing better, thank you.'

'Great,' said Justin. 'Where should we put P? He's sick. You should keep a tighter leash on him, Karen. You don't know where he's been, or who he's been with.'

Georgia's blood was ready to boil with frustration. Justin hadn't said a word on the short ride over, other than to warn her not to overplay her hand.

'The sofa in the family room.' Karen gestured over her shoulder, putting a hand to her head.

'I think he should go straight to bed, don't you, Justin? He's looking really peaky.' Georgia turned to look at Justin, who nodded.

'I'm going to take him up, Karen. Same room as usual?'

Karen nodded, starting towards the stairs. She led the way and stopped on the landing. Justin and Georgia stood waiting. There were four doors. The two on the left were open, as was the one on the right. The one behind her was closed, and there was a keypad on the door.

Georgia looked over Karen's shoulder. 'Oh look, Justin. Karen's got an office just like yours.'

Fear flashed across the other woman's face and Georgia knew that Justin had seen it too. He helped Paul to sit down on the floor, leaning him against the banister. 'Is that where P keeps his guns, Karen?' Justin asked quietly.

'No. It's my room.'

'What do you keep in there?' Georgia asked conversationally. 'Must be really important if you need a code to get in. Can I see?'

'No!' Karen exclaimed. 'I want you to leave. I'll look after Paul now. I'm sure you've got other things to do.'

'No, not really.' Georgia took a step toward her. 'What's so secret, Karen? What is it you've got hidden in there?'

'You wouldn't understand,' Karen spat, moving backward until she stood with her back to the door.

'Open the door, please?' Justin asked. Karen shook her head, her lip trembling.

'Open. That. Door,' he enunciated clearly. 'Now.'

Again she shook her head, beginning to slide down the door, curling herself into a ball.

Justin moved her aside and with a well-aimed kick, forced the door open. Georgia darted around him, reaching for the light switch, and gasped as light flooded the room.

There, surrounded by dozens of lifelike porcelain baby dolls, lay Misty.

Epilogue

Georgia sat on the back porch at Justin's house. It was the first time she'd been there since they'd found Misty. It was Misty's ninth birthday, and they were holding the party at Justin's because Misty and nine of her new friends wouldn't all fit in their own back yard.

Although a blood sample had been taken to prove Justin's paternity, they'd had no further conversation about it. Rather than getting hung up on the biology, though, Justin had gone ahead and built a great relationship with his daughter. Meanwhile, Georgia's own relationship with him remained complicated. They still hadn't really talked since all the revelations — she guessed Justin needed time to get his head around the sort of person his best friend had turned out to be. And also to adjust at work, since they'd permanently lost one of their team; Karen was now serving serious time. But they were going to have to talk soon.

'Mind if I sit?'

'It's your home.' Georgia shifted slightly and he sat down, laying his arm across the back of the padded bench.

Georgia turned her attention to the children as they laughed together, playing with the fantastic dolls' house Justin had bought her as a present. Georgia knew it would keep her daughter entertained for hours, exercising her imagination to its fullest. Misty's leg was healing, though it would still be some time before she could run around like she used to. She apparently remembered nothing of the accident, or anything of the few days following it. For that much, Georgia was eternally grateful.

The sheriff's department had found the same prefilled syringes at Karen's house that they had found in Tracy's medicine bag. They were traced back to the hospital, where Tracy had faked a prescription, lacing the coffee she had fetched for Georgia, and also keeping Misty sedated.

'I went to see Paul yesterday,' Justin said quietly.

'Oh?' Georgia still felt physically sick at the sound of his name.

'He's been sober for ninety days now. He's been having therapy to work through some issues.'

Georgia pressed her lips together and nodded. She couldn't care less about Paul and his issues.

'Remember the day we found Misty, you told me to ask him about the internal investigation?'

She looked at him properly for the first time in months. 'And?'

'He told me the truth. Just like you said, he'd been drinking before our shift, and he carried on drinking. He heard the gunshots, and he didn't go to their aid. He's been carrying guilt around for a long time.'

'Guilt for what? For the fact that two

men were murdered? For attacking me?'

'Both.'

'Wow.' Georgia knew she sounded sarcastic, but Justin didn't react.

'And he came clean about the night you left. Again, just like you said.'

Georgia tore her gaze away. She saw more in his eyes than she wanted to. She sat in silence and said simply, 'Okay.'

'I'm sorry I didn't believe you straight away. And I'm sorry you weren't able to come to me when it happened. I guess I never dealt with my feelings when you left, and then when you came back into my life, with those secrets, and with Misty, I . . . ' Justin's voice cracked slightly, and Georgia swallowed back tears that were trying so hard to fall.

'I'm sorry, too.' She turned slightly to face him. 'I should have stayed to work it all out.'

Justin took her hand and squeezed it. 'Look, I know it's Misty's birthday, but

I got you something too.' He reached into the inside pocket of his jacket and pulled out a manila envelope, saying with a wry smile, 'I admit it's not the prettiest of presents, but I hope you understand what it means.'

Georgia took the envelope, reading the front. It was addressed to Justin Rose. Turning it around, she saw there was a security seal on it, and it hadn't been opened.

'It's okay, you can go ahead and open it if you want to.'

Georgia opened the envelope, peering inside. There was a single sheet of paper. Pulling it out, she saw that it was from the hospital. The words *test result* swam before her eyes as tears pooled.

'I don't care what the test says, Georgia. I know I'm Misty's father. I didn't open it because I didn't need to. I trust you, and I love you. Both of you.'

Georgia showed him the wording on the result slip: *positive*.

Justin smiled and curled the arm he'd been resting along the back of the bench around her shoulders. 'I love you, hun. I never stopped.'

She lifted her face and smiled. 'I love you too, Justin.'

He grinned and pressed his lips to hers, gently but firmly.

'There is one more thing,' she whispered against his lips.

'No more secrets, please. Just tell me,' he whispered back.

Georgia giggled and put his hand on her belly. Her man's eyes widened. 'I've got a present for you too. By my reckoning, it should be due around Christmas!'

We do hope that you have enjoyed reading this large print book.

Did you know that all of our titles are available for purchase?

We publish a wide range of high quality large print books including:
Romances, Mysteries, Classics
General Fiction
Non Fiction and Westerns

Special interest titles available in large print are:
The Little Oxford Dictionary
Music Book, Song Book
Hymn Book, Service Book

Also available from us courtesy of Oxford University Press:
Young Readers' Dictionary
(large print edition)
Young Readers' Thesaurus
(large print edition)

For further information or a free brochure, please contact us at:
Ulverscroft Large Print Books Ltd.,
The Green, Bradgate Road, Anstey,
Leicester, LE7 7FU, England.
Tel: (00 44) 0116 236 4325
Fax: (00 44) 0116 234 0205

*Other titles in the
Linford Romance Library:*

A MOMENT LIKE THIS

Rena George

When Jenna Maitland's cousin Joss flees the responsibilities of their family's department store empire in Yorkshire, he escapes to Cornwall to follow his true calling and paint. Accompanied by the mysterious Gil Ryder, Jenna sets off south to find him. Once in Cornwall, Jenna finds herself becoming increasingly attracted to Gil — but is warned off by the attractive Victoria Symington, who appears to regard Gil as her own. Meanwhile, Joss's whereabouts has been discovered — but he is refusing to return . . .

BROKEN PROMISES

Chrissie Loveday

The greatest day of Carolyn's life has arrived: she is to marry her beloved Henry. But when she gets to the church, it becomes clear that something is terribly wrong. The groom has disappeared! Devastated, Carolyn is supported by her brother and his girlfriend as she tries to pick up the pieces of her life. When she meets kind, caring Jed, she feels as if she really is over Henry — but is this just a rebound? And will she ever find out why she was jilted at the altar?